Tag Alder Tales

For my wife Rhonda,
who has made the years since I first met her
the best years of my life.

Also by Charlie Smith:

The Beast that God has Kissed: Songs from the Birch Lake Road (YSP, 2000)

Through Three Long Miles of Night: More Songs from the Birch Lake Road (YSP, 2003)

Acknowledgements

Some of these stories have appeared in, or been read on, *Highgrader Magazine* and CBC Northern Ontario Radio.

Tag Alder Tales

by

Charlie Smith

Your Scrivener Press

Library and Archives Canada Cataloguing in Publication

Smith, Charlie, 1948-
Tag alder tales / Charlie Smith.

Short stories.
ISBN 1-896350-15-1

1. Country life — Ontario, Northern — Fiction.
2. Ontario, Northern — Fiction. I. Title.

PS8587.M5242T34 2005 C813'.6 C2005-902044-X

Book design: Laurence Steven
Cover design: Chris Evans
Interior illustrations: John Vary

Published by *Your Scrivener Press*
465 Loach's Road,
Sudbury, Ontario, Canada, P3E 2R2
info@yourscrivenerpress.com
www.yourscrivenerpress.com

Contents

Tourists in Burpee

In Evansville, in Burpee Township on the Manitoulin Island, there was a time when the sun shone all summer long and the moon at night cast shadows over dreams. I was as free then as a bird in flight, unfettered by school in the summer or parents' worry in the fall. The only cautions I had were those of kinship, speeding drunks and the cops.

"Cobs!" they called them. We would ring a general on the old crank phones: "Cobs are coming up the Blind Line!" They meant cops. I don't know why they called them Cobs, I didn't, but the Pattersons did, and so did most of my friends. Game Wardens also caught our interest. You could feel a wave of tension sweeping through the township like a chill. "Did you hear? The Warden nabbed Blain!"

"No! Son-of-a-bitch!"

Now even if we lived in Burpee township, we said we lived in Evansville, which was our post office address. There really was no Evansville left, not when I was a kid. I guess you could say there was a place

7

that Evansville used to be, and there was a dot on the map, but seeing as Pete Bell's store, switch, post office, gas station and chicken shoot location had burned to its single footings, and that across the road the one room public school with its dozen and a half students was due to close down soon, and that across the corner the old rickety Burpee Hall (they said the Law had shut her down) had not even a sign for the wind to swing, and that there were four houses in all, the farmers from the quarter sections and one son just come back — I'd guess you couldn't even call Evansville a hamlet anymore. We had lost that distinction.

Occasionally a tourist would pull up beside me and ask, "Where is Evansville?"

"Right here!" I'd say, as if I were announcing a circus act.

The tourist would usually have a map, which is where he was led wrong in the first place; roads that were on the map were now impassible, towns were faded to gray and had sunk into weedy deserted lots. Directions were always given vaguely: "Drive west, till you come to where Pete Bell's Store used to be, then turn left on the Blind Line."

Of course there were no signs, and there the poor soul would be, worrying about the paint on his new shiny '56 Ford, his wife pissed off, his kids crying, his guts grumbling and his manhood diminished, with that stupid old map from the war survey; and as if fate wasn't being unkind enough to him, he'd stop and ask me.

I'd see him coming. I'd look down the side road and spot the poor bastard before he was much more than a speck being stalked by a huge cloud of white dust. The sun would glint on the new paint progressing slowly and before I even could see the head swiveling wildly around I knew I had a tourist coming. If I wasn't already chewing tobacco I'd make sure I had a good wet one working around when he got there.

"Gooday!" I'd say, with as wet and wild a smile as a chewing ten year old can manage. Now I have to admit right here, that I wasn't as good at it as Bev Patterson; he could reduce them to near tears of derision with one little polished "Gooday!" But he had it down to an art, often didn't wear shoes and had the advantage of a somewhat big head.

"What'ya mean?" The tourist would wave his sweat-stained map at me. "I'm looking for Evansville."

"You found it!" About then I would spit in the dusty gravel with about as much force as possible without actually hawking. "Aye, this is it!"

Now this is where the poor old tourist would sort of lose control. It was sad really; I mean if he'd actually relaxed a bit he would have appreciated the drama of my little show—he'd have laughed at this on the big screen. I'd wave around as if it was a panorama, and I guess it was. "This here," I'd say, "is Evansville!"

The wife would sort of screw up her face and lean over. You could see by her expression (it was always the same) that there was no sense letting her husband muck up this vacation any further. "We are looking for the town of Evansville."

This was my cue to go over to her side of the car; the female of the tourist was more fun even than the male. I'd try to let a little tobacco juice gather on the corner of my mouth. The windows would all be down of course; I'd saunter around, kicking rocks with my big old work boots, and glance in at the kids, some of them as old or older than me. Kids are harder to B.S. than adults; the best way is just to ignore them, then they pay really close attention. If they had a dog though, I'd immediately identify him.

"Say, isn't that a Cocker Spaniel? Yep, it is; an American! Is he any good for birds?" What a damn hypocrite I was. I knew full well that strange tourist people always had a dog, and never used him for his intended purpose. If it was a boxer, I'd ask, "Do you fight him?" By now they are all so sick of the hyper dog crammed into the back with the kids that they would like to get rid of him, but didn't want to start that line of thinking or the kids would go too.

I'd yatter on to them about dogs, admire their car, anything to stretch out the conversation as long as possible. Some of my friends were scared of them; not that they were really afraid, they just didn't want to talk too much to strangers. It certainly never crossed my mind that I might get kidnapped or anything. I always figured that taking me was about the farthest thing from their minds; none even offered me a ride up the long white road. "Where you folks from?"

They were either from Michigan, Ohio or Southern Ontario, and the poor "outsiders" were just trying to get through our becursed township to get to some tourist lodge or something, and some sadist had sent them off onto the backroads of the Island. "How did you get here?" I'd ask.

Now if they had any brains they would say to me that someone had steered them wrong. If that was the case I'd usually draw them a quick map in the dust, and instruct them to "Back up, turn around, go down that road till you come to the highway, and don't leave it again! Oh, west is to the left!"

Sometimes though I had an adventurer, a cross country kind of guy. "Let's see some new country dear! We went by the highway last year!"

If that was the kind of fellow I was dealing with — The Shortcut Kid — I'd give more cryptic directions: Go on up west, turn north, then turn west again. Which was correct, but even though the sun was always beating down, and all the roads ran to the cardinal directions, these poor hapless city people could not tell up from down. Mind you, I'd point, and I am sure that they all eventually got out. Except once in a while there would be another car hauled out on the "prairie" burns to rot, so...no, no, they all got out. But I'd make them work at it, turn his map around here and there, squint, ask questions.

It was good for them.

"Tourists!" We said it then like it was a bit of an insult. They weren't kin of ours, and their customs were not ours, and everytime I looked at them, I saw the future, and I think so did my friends. We tanned lads of the back roads — disheveled, slouch-hatted, tobacco-chewing, smoke-rolling little outlaws — I figure we knew every time we saw them, saw them looking at us, driving by looking at our fathers' farms, laughing, staring, coveting, deriding and never understanding. "Tourists!" we said, meaning all of that.

We used to walk, bike, ride, motorscooter down to Bill Middaugh's store, five miles down around a corner by the lake, houses nestling in, cottages on the shore, a couple of resorts and fast becoming "Evansville," although by my reckoning it should have been called Middaugh.

Bill Middaugh had everything I wanted: ice-cream — chocolate, vanilla, strawberry — five cents a scoop, pop eight cents, tobacco and papers thirty-five cents, chewing tobacco a quarter — Stag, Big Ben, and another weaker one that I never bought. The .22 shorts were fifty-five cents a box, long rifle (which I reserved for deer) were eighty-five cents.

We would hang around there for an hour or so, it being a fair hike to home. In the summer we'd go down to Campbell's Bay and swim; as a matter of fact that was what passed for a bath for us. But first we'd go to Bill Middaugh's store. We must have been ripe after the five hot miles in the sun.

Now I had lived outside Burpee Township, so I knew we talked funny, with a bit of a Scots accent and old fashioned. I used to love standing out there in a bunch, looking for all the world like the too-young remnants of an 1890 recruiting drive, and watch the tourists watching us. "Gooday!" Bev would say as they drew abreast of our line; it was often too much for them. When they laughed at us, I always acted outraged. "What's wrong Mr.? Is something funny?" and I'd spit close to their loafer shoes.

If one of them had answered the bunch of us, "You! I am laughing at you, you inbred little hillbillies!" we would have melted like snow, but it never happened; they were always embarrassed — and they should have been because they destroyed us.

Watching Maudie Load

Maudie Campbell was her name. Her dad, Old Man Campbell, owned the biggest, the best farm around here. He had the first haybine, the first round baler, the first imported French bulls and he had Maudie, no son, no other daughter, just Maudie.

The Campbells were really religious; not Black Socks, as we called one of the local, small religious sects, but something else. I forget right off what the hell it was, could have been Baptist, I don't know. Dad always called them Holy Rollers, whatever that was supposed to be. Whatever they were, they were hard working frugal folks, not much set to putting on airs, unless the newest of equipment could be translated as prideful, and I suppose it could.

Do you remember the Massey 35 tractor? Quite cutting edge it was at the time, it and the bigger models like it. Nothing fancy by today's standards. We would call them underpowered and too small, crude even. But at the time when the rest of us were making due with old International H's, Cockshutts, and such, well in those days the Massey 35 with its diesel engine, live power take off, all hydraulic loader and three point hitch was our hearts' desire. It could have had something to do with the ads on the Don Messer show: "Turn up the power at the flip of a switch, turn down the dieselage for power. Come buy the tractor and enjoy the switch to Massey Ferguson Multi Power." Or it could have been the toy tractors that the Massey dealer sprinkled around the townships at special events. Whatever the reason, we all thought that the Canadian made Massey was the tractor to have.

Old Man Campbell bought a Massey 35 and set Maudie to picking up round bales with it, loading them eleven at a time on a wagon and hauling them into place in long rows in the bale park. I hear she also cut hay with it in the morning, but all I ever watched was Maudie load.

Now Maudie wasn't much of a looker, plain I guess would be the best way to describe her, a bit too square in the stance, too square in the jaw, and well, too square. She used to wear calf-length print dresses and white socks when the other girls were wearing mini-skirts and shorts. She had blond hair but it was coarse and usually tied back in a serviceable bun. Her hands were red and callused like a man's. She was somewhat muscley, which gave her an overweight appearance, at least next to the other girls who never did anything more strenuous than wash the occasional sink full of dishes.

Maudie on the tractor was a different thing. I heard about it the first time from Pete, who said he and Harold had been driving along the third concession when he saw Macgregor's half ton truck parked by the side of the road, with young Fred sitting in it watching someone pick up bales. Fred is a good sort, if a bit ginky, so the boys pulled over to have a gab. He was friendly enough, Pete said, but secretive, sort of like a dog with a juicy bone hidden when he doesn't want to let on he has something to hide.

It was August and most of us had our haying done. Not the Campbells. They ran a hundred cows, so they hayed longer than most of us, and of course all those bales out in the field had to be picked up sometime, into September even, although it was supposedly easier, what with their state of the art equipment and all. Well, all of us square bale throwers were on a well-deserved rest, and Pete and Harold stuck around to see what Fred was hiding.

Poor Fred, he couldn't keep from turning his head, and when the boys followed his look, they noticed Maudie loading bales.

"You got to see this!" was all that Pete would say.

How can I explain the metamorphosis that I saw in Maudie the next day, when I joined the pickups and cars parked along the third concession? Poetry in motion, girl and machine working in smooth interdependence, never a ground gear, never a wasted motion. Maudie was wearing a white cowboy hat, jeans and a long sleeved light cotton shirt. She had on sunglasses. She wore glasses anyway but somehow the sunglasses gave her a more mysterious, vampish look. I knew damn well she had no makeup on, but her naturally fair complexion, the sun and I suppose the heat from the humming red tractor made her cheeks glow and her lips moist and red. The shirt would press against her lithe muscles, or the pert breasts. My God, like Pete said, "You had to see it."

The tractor would rock over the dead furrows. She would roll in the seat in easy dominance of it, and of the spear on the front of the loader. She would caress the levers and it would obey her touch. All on the move: the swoop and dive of the loader, the bale picked up on the fly, the tight turn, the bale placed on the wagon, the others on top straddling the bottom row, Maudie straddling the tractor, the tractor obeying her every whim.

Everyone could see Fred was some mad at us all being there. But what could he say? Apparently, so the rumor went, he had been sitting there watching Maudie load for three days on and off. Well, not there really, he had followed the show from field to field, sometimes too far to see anything but the smooth dance of the machine and driver, but sometimes close enough to exchange the odd look. Very odd, I'd bet.

Fred could have been a good looking lad had it not been that his parents were too practical and poor to waste money fixing up a set of perfectly serviceable, if crooked teeth, and had he a chin and a shorter neck to set it on. But even then he would still have had that stupid yuck yuck voice. Still, Fred had seen her first and must have had aspirations because he didn't much like us all hanging around, but what could he say?

"Oh, another crow for the fence, yuck yuck," he said to me when I came. To hell with him; he didn't scare me even a little bit.

"She knows she is being watched," said Harold.

"Well of course she knows; she isn't stupid." Pete grinned and wiggled his fingers toward her.

"No, I mean she's performing." Harold tilted his

head thoughtfully. "See the exaggerated movements, the way she sways in the seat when she crosses the dead furrow? She's performing."

"To hell with you!" said Fred, which was a trifle bold, seeing as Harold could have eaten his head like a French fry. "Yuck yuck," he added, to take the edge off.

I could see that Fred was powerfully irked, so I grinned at him. "See the way she sort of slows her hand down after shifting gears, just as it passes the seat. See how she rests it on her thigh?"

"Oh, she's getting off on it all right," Bob sneered, "and so am I."

Wes made a comment that went too far, and the next thing you know we were holding the two of them apart and Fred was threatening all sorts of violent things.

When we went back to school I expected that there would be some holdover of the glamour in Maudie, the raw sexiness. But no, she was the same shy dowdy girl she had always been. The only sign she ever gave of any awareness of her fan club was when she momentarily met the eye of one of the many interested parties; then she would blush and look down. Fred seemed always to be hovering near her, at class change, at lunchtime. I don't think they ever spoke, or even exchanged shy glances, but he was always close.

On the weekends though, she was still Maudie the Loader. That's what we called her. "There's Fred looking moony; Maudie the Loader must be close."

On any warm afternoon you could find some of us whiling away some time watching her load, that is until one day Old Man Campbell drove past slow, stopped his truck, backed up, and rolled down the window. We expected hollering, but he just asked, "Can I help you boys?"

We didn't want any of his help. We didn't exactly know what his help might be, so we blushed, said our good days, shuffled off to our vehicles and left. All but Fred; the last I saw of him he was leaning on the fender of Old Man Campbell's truck, yuck yucking away.

Fred still went to watch Maudie load. The rest of us didn't. Now Fred drove right into the yard, and went out into the field with his own 8N Ford pulling another wagon. She would load both of them, and then he would hold the tongue on Maudie's wagon when it came time for her to hitch (even though she didn't need it, for she could back up fast and stop in the right spot for the pin). He ate meals with them, helped Old Man Campbell with the cattle and such, more or less worked there.

Fred and Maudie got married young, right out of high school, about two summers after we first noticed her loading I guess. They farm down the road from me, have two kids now. Fred joined the same church as them, but he was never much of a wildcat anyway, fit right in I suppose.

A lot of years have gone by since then. They inherited her dad's farm, and bought another when they were young, but you know, it's funny, when the rest of us went to the big, big round bales, Fred didn't. He still uses that little 4 X 4 type, and when he is done baling, say when it's too damp, he still sits in the field, his arms folded on his steering wheel, and watches Maudie load.

Calf

His name was Cal, but his father used to say to him, "You're just like a Charolais calf!" So we all called him "Calf."

I don't know if you know much about cattle, but a Charolais calf is big, blond and stupid. That's what he was like. A Charolais calf can find the tit alright, if you put it in his mouth, maybe a couple of times. Other breeds of cattle aren't like that—the Shorthorn for instance—which is just as well because any Shorthorn cows I ever had were so damn protective that you couldn't get anywhere near their calves. Those Scots must have been cattle thieves. His mother was a Scot, and she was as protective of him as any Shorthorn cow. Angus calves are smart and kind of wild, or maybe it's the wildness that makes them smart, but they get up right away and find their own damn tit, thank you very much, keep your hands to yourself. And that's what his father was like, but not him. No, he was like a Charolais calf; you had to show him how to do everything. Things his brothers used to just up and do, he had to study.

"See, this is the clutch!" His father figured out that's how you had to teach him, even if his younger brothers had already crawled all over the thing, and could have driven it, which they would have done if they hadn't been so scared of the old man. And that changed as soon as their father figured out that they could drive a lot better than Calf ever would.

Calf was better looking than they were, in a tall, Nordic sort of way. With his muscles all bunched over his strung-out frame, you'd have almost bet he could outwork them, his brothers or his father, but you would have been wrong. I suppose he could lift more; only problem is, work isn't a lifting competition, it's a steady grind. I guess that's why we never called him Ox or Bull, because an ox or a bull will really work at something (for bad or for good), but Calf could never quite get motivated.

Kids used to get into fights with him. He wasn't a pushover; after all, he was always the biggest kid in the class, but he wasn't really strong and he was kind of soft. He didn't look soft, but he was. Somebody about three parts his size would poke him in the beak, and he'd cry like a big baby. Of course then he'd get mad, but then nobody wanted to fight with him, and he'd just stand there and bawl.

He did alright though. He was smart enough I guess, if he was carefully tended. He did good in school, just the boy those teachers were looking for — a malleable personality, friendly and outgoing. "Cal is having another good year," his mother would say, handing the old man his report card.

The old fart would look at it, the rows of A's, the

glowing comments, then sort of sigh, and say, "That's very good son."

"Here are Bob and Bill's." She'd hold them out to him. Every semester, the same thing.

"Yah, yah," the old man would say, or something like that. "Are they going to pass?"

Every time she would grudgingly admit that, "Yes they are, but look at these marks, and these behaviour comments."

And every year he would grumble, "That's good enough," or, "They'll do alright!" and that was the end of it.

I figure that Bob and Bill could have damn near kissed him. They'd look across the table to where Calf sat beside his mother and as far away from the old man as he could get without sitting on the other end of the table, which was where their sister sat. Of course Bill was across from him and just as far away from the old man, but that was only because Bob was bigger and he wanted to sit beside their father.

Calf more or less ignored them, directing any conversation to his sister or his mother, and if necessary their father. He seldom spoke to Bob or Bill except to say, "Pass the potatoes please." He always said "please," "thank you," and, "you're welcome." And he used to insist that he was in charge, because he was the eldest. There they'd be out picking up bales, he'd be building the load, Bob and Bill would be moving the tractor and throwing on stooks of bales, and he'd be standing up there giving orders: "Get that one over there, please Bill."

Of course as often as not his ideas were stupid. Bob and Bill would tell him so, or just ignore him, and he'd sort of sob, "I'm the oldest, I'm in charge!" He even said it when he was eighteen or so, and it was damn obvious that they were going to do whatever the hell they wanted, because after all they were better at it than him. It made him look like...well, like a bleating calf.

One spring, when the shoulders were soft, Old Frank and I met him on the road. We were in a half ton and he was driving a tractor—no load or anything—just a two-wheel drive loader tractor, an International 474. He pulled way over, waved at us on the way by, and got stuck with the damn thing. "So help me God," said Old Frank, "the silly bastard just got stuck, on the road, with a tractor!"

By the time Old Frank and I got over to him, he'd tried to back up, cramped his front wheels, and got the loader spear stuck in the ground. "Hold it, for Christ's sakes!" hollers Old Frank. "You're going to upset the damn thing! Either let me drive or get in with us and we'll take you to get your old man or one of your brothers." Old Frank looked at the tractor sitting there buried up to the hub on the low side. "Maybe he better bring another tractor. You tell him that I said so."

We let him off at their lane. "You know," said Old Frank as Calf walked out of ear shot, "I always thought you needed a Charolais bull to make a Charolais calf. Don't you?"

And yah, I'd often thought the same thing, everybody had. But nobody mentioned it to his old man, not any more, anyway.

It was obvious that Calf was never going to make a farmer, his old man told him that right up. He said it

when Calf was just finishing grade thirteen and it was
report card time again, and his mother was handing
the old man the report card, with its perfect marks.
"Cal is going to go to university!" his mother had
announced.

"Good!" said the old man. "I think it's a good idea.
Cal you're never going to make a farmer."

The mother had expected an argument; she sort of
deflated. "Good then, that's settled."

"Yep," said the old man. "Of course we can only
afford to send one to university; Dolores is already
married, so Bob and Bill will get the farm."

The mother's eyes snapped. "What about Cal?"

"He gets university."

That's Bob and Bill's farm right over there. See the
new addition on the barn, and the pit silo? They're
doing okay those boys. Bought Old Frank's place too;
they needed a separate house anyway, once Bob got
married. Bill just lived at home single until the old man
died and his mother moved to the nursing home. Then
he got married too.

I felt sorry for the old woman leaving the farm and
moving into a place like that, but it's in the city right
close to where Calf has his office, and he comes and
sees her every day.

No, the one I feel sorry for is Calf. See, in the end
the old man screwed up his life. The conniving old
bastard must have known all his life that Calf wasn't
his kid. He'd married a pregnant woman who said it
was, but he was no fool; it had to be as obvious to him
as to the rest of the township. It wasn't poor Calf's
fault, and the old man never suggested it was, nor I

don't suppose did he ever say anything to his wife—
but the thing he did to Calf ruined him. He ruined
him because he never hit him, when maybe a cuff up
alongside the head might have woken that kid up. He
ruined him by letting him off any job that Calf found
too trying—"Dad, do you mind if I do something else,
please."

He could have made a man out of him. Calf didn't
have to be stuck in that Goddamned city, taking a
vacation somewhere every once in a while, just to get
some air and sun, wasting his life buying silly luxuries,
married twice, divorced twice, and living in the
shadow of a tower of humanity.

Meanwhile back on the farm there are Bob and Bill.
Oh sure, they don't make a lot of money, and yes, once
or twice they've had to borrow from him. As a matter
of fact he is now a silent partner; he keeps the books
for them too I think, and they're doing okay. But poor
Calf, there he is spending his whole life behind a desk,
while Bob and Bill get to be farmers.

Terry

We went to school together, back in sixty-five. I never thought that he would amount to much. I don't think anybody else did either. It's hard to say what made us all think of him like that. There was nothing outwardly wrong with him, or different, and as you may well recall the two things were interchangeable back then. He was not tall, or short. He was not fat, nor was he a bone rack. He had no more pimples than the rest of us, and was as devoid of body odour as any self-conscious teenage boy.

I never knew him to go out on a date, but then I didn't actually burn up the old social registry either. He was not a scholarly brown-noser, which was what we goof-ups thought the kids in the five-year program were. He didn't say anything in class, but hell, that could just as easily be said about most of the misfits in my crowd.

It would be Friday afternoon, and Old Johnson would be droning on about cosigns or some other God awful boring thing, and meanwhile the fall sun would be beaming down on those big walls of glass, and you'd know that the partridge would be sunning themselves on the hill sides. Your dad and your uncles would be harvesting the dusty rich grain. Well, your attention would wander, naturally, then the next thing you knew you'd be looking down at Sue Ann's well trimmed ankles, and wondering what lay above. Stuff like that. You'd look over and there he'd be with that same disinterested glaze on his eyes that he always had. It made you want to ball up some paper and whack him alongside the head. But if you did (and probably got caught) he'd pay no more attention than if a fly had landed on him.

We were mean often. You were a kid once, so I am sure you understand. We meant no harm really. Well at least I didn't, but it was a challenge. I just wanted to get through to him, get some reaction other than that stupid glazed look. He looked like he was studying something in behind those eyes — "Yoo hoo, are you in there?"

The funny thing is, he got good marks. Oh, nothing that would elevate him up into the five year plan where he might have to wake up or anything, but for a guy that never did homework and didn't participate in class at all, he did pretty good, and that was galling. There I'd be struggling to understand what the teacher was talking about, even lugging books home occasionally, and I'd just scrape by. But he always got in the high sixties-low seventies, as if that was a safe place to hide.

That was what he was doing. Hiding. I am not an academic or anything, but I'm not as dumb as I look, and I have seen that same expression on range cattle, when you finally get them in the chute, and there is no place left to run. I have seen it once on the face of a wounded deer, same look, the look of an animal that has no escape, no fight left in it so it just hides somewhere in behind the eyes.

There is no mercy in nature for a wounded animal, and there is not much mercy in a bunch of teenage boys. We thought we were a pretty rough bunch, and for sure, even if none of us could put a name to that look, we all recognized it, and were on him like a pack of dogs at a poor helpless sheep. The dogs aren't hungry, the sheep is no contest or game — it is just that they are trying to get one more response from the poor thing.

He was tough, if a total lack of reaction can be called tough. Maybe numb would be a better word. I saw Harold ball up his big muscley fist and punch him right in the gut, for no reason. For all I know, maybe his old man had yelled at him at home, so to take it out he just suckered poor Terry. Terry kind of leaned over for a beat or two and stood against the lockers, then he took a deep breath, straightened up and walked to his next class. "Hell," Harold said, "he was hard — like hitting the side of a bull or something." That gained Terry some grudging respect.

He rode on my bus, got on pretty early at the school, and sat up near the front. He must have had some instinct for survival because he got bothered less up there — up with the girls. But if the driving was bad and old Harrison had to concentrate on keeping the damn thing between the snowbanks, someone would sit behind Terry and flick his ears — flick, flick, flick — until they were cherry red. Even a little grade nine could do it. Come to think of it, it was usually some little twerp. It didn't matter. Poor Terry would just sit there looking out the window as if he was going to a concentration camp or something. This would go on until the kid got bored with flicking him, Harrison noticed, or one of us big guys told his tormenter to bug off.

I knew his family, sort of. They were perfectly normal as far as I could see. His sister was older, but his brother was in grade ten, and just a regular guy — the same look, only the lights were on in the kitchen. He told me once that Terry lifted weights when not working on the farm. I guess that was his one defense, and an explanation why he could take a punch like that. Not that he excelled at track or hockey or anything. Maybe he could have, but he didn't try unless Coach made him, and then he just ran in the middle of the pack. Say we were doing push-ups. As soon as about half the guys reached their limit and just lay there on their bellies, pooped out, he'd quit too. Coach caught on one time and yelled at him, "Give me some more!" Terry didn't even shrug, he just kept doing push–ups for the rest of gym class, while poor old failed athletic Coach stood there with his jaw hanging open.

I don't want to give you the ida that he was a superman bodybuilder or something. No, his brother said that he never tried hard enough to get really good. There were lots of guys in school stronger than him, probably. You wouldn't have known at all though, unless you'd seen the push-ups or big Harold punch him in the gut.

I told him one time that I thought he might have

been able to take Harold—that in my considered opinion Harold wasn't all that tough (although I sure as hell wouldn't have wanted to try him). But anyway, why didn't he hit him back? If someone is hitting you anyway. I mean, it takes two to make a fight, otherwise it's just a beating. He looked at me with those listless eyes, and I had the feeling that I wouldn't want him coming at me with that couldn't-t-care-less-for-nothing-in-this-world look on his face. I'd rather fight Harold any day.

After that I got to watching him closer. I half expected him to come to school with a shotgun and kill all of us. Of course it didn't happen. I also thought maybe he would kill himself, but that never happened either. What did happen is a lot weirder, and is what I am wasting your time trying to tell you.

Now this was the time before spot checks, and the war on drunk driving. Just as well, because when we weren't being bused into town and educated or working like apprentice hired hands at home we were out raising hell. We drove an assortment of Dads' trucks or our own beat-up wrecks. Dances in those days were rough affairs. There was always one where nobody danced at all.

All the townships were dry, which was a damn lie. We'd get an older brother to bring us a bottle or we'd borrow a vehicle and go into town and get a rubby to buy us some booze. Then off we'd go, a bunch of us crammed in a rustbucket to whatever hall had the dance at the time.

There was lots of drinking outside in the trucks, or safer yet, in the bush behind the hall; pretty soon inside you'd go with maybe just enough courage to ask some wallflower to dance. Oh, the dance—out on the floor with the fathers and mothers, while the four-piece band on the stage sawed away at schottisches, polkas as square dances (which we never participated in), and waltzes and stuff like that which we seldom did. Instead, we stood around in the back of the hall and got steadily drunker. Personally, by the time I ever worked up enough courage and intoxication to ask anyone to dance, I was so damn plastered that anyone I would want to dance with would have nothing to do with me.

There was the odd fight, of course. You couldn't have that many frustrated young farmers—all with a complete knowledge of how sex worked, at least in an agricultural sense, yet lacking the social grace required to get us there—without the stew of alcohol and testosterone boiling over from time to time. You've seen fights like that—a lot of yapping, then some pushing, both men not really wanting to fight, then a punch or two and a lot of wrestling as everybody pulls them apart. Big heroes, "I kicked his ass!" etc.

There was always one dance that was known as the fighting dance. They had a band, but God knows why! Nobody danced. They should have piped in Wagner—not that any of us would have recognized it. I was never a fighter, never really liked the idea of the humiliation and the pain of it. Maybe I was chicken, maybe I had no big urge to hurt anyone. I don't know. But I went. If you were careful and stuck with a bunch of guys from your township or your school, or maybe your kin, you could usually get away with it. Keep your mouth shut and watch the show. There was a certain prestige in just surviving one of those dances.

You'd walk in from the cold, behind the biggest guy in your bunch, with your collar turned up around your neck and your sleeves rolled up. Somebody would yell, "Fred, Pete, Harold, over here!" and you'd go and stand in a knot with a bunch of your buddies. You'd see maybe four, five fights all going on at once, or maybe none at all. Entertainment was not guaranteed.

I am just telling you all this so you will understand what our social life was like — bloody noses, black eyes. No one ever really badly hurt; not at that time, at least.

I don't know why Terry came to the dance. Could be that his brother brought him. They came in together. Terry had been drinking; I could see that. It kind of surprised me a little, like catching my collie killing a chicken. Despite the fact that we all drank, we thought there was something a little risky about it. Come to think of it, I guess the way we did it there was. Anyway, old Terry was in the bag. I could smell it on him halfway across the room. Cheap rye, right out of the bottle, no doubt still in the liquor store bag (our clever disguise).

Now the funny thing about Terry drunk was, well, he sort of woke up. His eyes sparkled, and he walked right across the middle of that tense hall, right down the scuffed hardwood, came right up to my face and said, "Good day. How's it going?"

Well, it was going strange with me, as you can gather. I'm not a quiet type of lad, but I damn near swallowed my tongue. "Terry, what the hell are you doing here?"

Terry was quite chatty, for Terry at least, but he didn't say anything of great importance — like I sort of thought he would. Instead, he just stood there, swaying

and breathing whisky fumes on the rest of us, with a
big silly grin on his face.

Pete nudged me; I looked up to see Bug tacking
over toward us. I don't know what Bug's last name
was, or his real first name for that matter. Everybody
just called him Bug. I always thought it was because
he was always bugging someone, but it could have
been because he was such an obnoxious, ugly, bloated
piece of human garbage. I hoped that he wasn't aiming
at me. I found myself drifting a little closer to Harold,
for even if Bug was a fighter, he wasn't a complete
fool. I saw Pete retreat a step or two and try to get
Terry's attention, but Terry just stood there yattering
away about some fool thing, and even smiled right in
Bug's ugly face.

"Do you see something funny?"

Terry didn't even blink, though Bug was right in
his face. He just smiled a bit broader.

"How would you like a slap in the yap?" asked
Bug as way of greeting.

"Sure," says Terry, just like that, sort of cheerful
like, "Sure."

I could see that sort of set Bug back a little. He didn't
know Terry from Adam. Bug didn't go to our school.
Probably he didn't go to any school. He probably
thought that grade eight was lots of education. He no
doubt wanted to fight with this mild looking stranger,
but he expected some elaborate escalation of insult
first. He proceeded to call Terry names, most of them
lacking imagination. Hell, we had all baited old Terry
better than that with no reaction at all. Still, this was a
different Terry, and even though he wasn't just staring
blankly as usual, I expected some sort of avoidance

from him.

Now if it had been Pete or me that that obnoxious son of a bitch was baiting, Harold would most likely have said something to Bug, but it was Terry. He was not really a member of our clique, and I suppose that Harold was as curious as the rest of us as to how it would all turn out.

It appeared that Bug didn't know what to do. He stood there in front of Terry with his vocabulary all run out. He sort of looked around to make sure everybody had seen his little performance.

"Well," said Terry, "we don't have anything left to talk about do we?" and he turned and walked away. Poor Bug couldn't think of any retort. It looked for a second as if he was going to run after Terry and hit him in the back of the head, but he looked at Harold and changed his mind.

"Geek!" shouted Bug as way of leave-taking, and went back to join his buggy cousins on the other side of the hall. Personally, I'd had enough excitement, and I guess so had Harold and Pete. We shuffled out the door, retrieved our bottle from behind a pine tree and climbed in Pete's daddy's truck to leave. The last I saw of Terry that night was his brother holding him while he chucked his cookies over the side of the step railing. Our lights swung across him, and he lifted up his poor sorry head. I swear to God, he gave us a big silly grin. That was a grim sight.

I must be an idiot. I thought that come Monday, Terry would be a changed man. The wonder of modern chemistry, a sort of Dr. Jekyll and Mr. Hyde, or whatever. Alas, it was not to be! He was the same old Terry, only with somewhat bloodshot eyes.

Harold must have been thinking along the same lines; he shouted across the hall, "I thought you were going to actually fight that stupid Bug."

Terry didn't respond at all. He just stood there by his locker with a binder under his arm and that old listless look on his face. Harold shrugged. "Oh well, the damn fool wasn't worth fighting anyway."

"Hey!" said a holier-than-thou type from grade thirteen. "Didn't you clowns hear that Bug was killed in a car accident on Saturday night?"

"No," Harold stammered, "I didn't mean..."

The five year wonder started giving him a hard time about being unkind to the dead or something. Not that Harold could have possibly heard the news. The paper didn't come out till Wednesday, and all Harold heard on his father's farm was the same as I heard on mine—cows bawling. Cows don't gossip much and have a small centre of interest. Harold was busy trying to explain to the guy how he really didn't know. I figured the jerk already had that figured out and was just enjoying giving someone shit—someone who under different circumstances could have broken him like a twig.

I looked across to see what Terry thought of all this, but he just swept across me with those care-nothing eyes and walked down the hall toward our home room. I caught up with him as he was sitting down right in the middle of the classroom (a cruel joke pulled on him by the alphabet). My desk was over two rows and ahead—no alphabetic position this, but a fate forced on me by Old Johnson in pure spite, or some psychotic need to have me close. I sat on the edge of Terry's desk. "Did you know Bug was dead?"

He shook his head almost imperceptibly, but those eyes said, "I don't know, I don't care. Leave me alone!" So I did, but I felt funny about it.

I didn't see Terry come out of his shell again for nearly a month. By then it was deer season — the prime time of year for most of us. We had gone from waiting for Santa Claus to waiting for deer season with hardly a catch. Come opening morning, there would hardly be a boy in school. Tuesday a few would trickle back, most of them with deer stories to tell and a load of prestige to carry. By Thursday there would be enough boys in school, along with most of the girls, that it made sense to teach lessons again.

I had already shot a deer before the season. Of course I couldn't brag about it until well after, when we would be sitting around talking to the hot shots who got theirs legally. I had taken opening day anyway, but my old man said that was all I could have to hunt, seeing as my "lessons," as he called them, were doing so poorly.

Tuesday just Terry and I were there with most of the girls. I felt out of place. Hell, even some of the girls were out hunting, and there I was with that crew of misfits. It was a waste of time, anyway. All we did was review. My mind was so much on hunting, I didn't even bother flirting with the girls, despite having them pretty much to myself.

By Wednesday it was easier to take. Pete came back — all full of stories about the big doe he'd shot. The girls were all back and a couple of other guys. The five year classes were now all full. Those suck ups never took more than a day or two off, even for the rites of autumn. Pete was going on and on about his damn old gunky doe, and saying that his old man said he could have Friday off too, if their family didn't fill their tags. This gave me a ray of hope. Maybe I could swing the same kind of deal. My uncles from the south had lost some of their hunting instinct and so far had shot nothing. I told Pete this, but before he could answer Terry interrupted. "I might give it a try myself. Yep, I got a license two years ago." Pete and I must have looked funny, for he laughed, "I can hunt you know. Dad made me at first, but I got to kind of enjoy it." He grinned — as if to show that he too could love the crisp, cold mornings and the pounding heart of "Here comes one now!"

Terry was communicating — such a rare event that Old Johnson must have given us some leeway because it was nine-thirty when I looked at the clock. Too bad, because the old fart hadn't said anything up until he saw that I'd spotted the time. Then he cleared his throat and told us to take our seats. By that time, I'd learned more about Terry than I had in the preceding four years. He had a dog that was very good with cattle. He didn't like autoloading rifles or Massey tractors. He thought that Sue Ann was cute — a statement that she overheard and blushed at, but looked the rest of the day at Terry as if she was much more complimented than when I had screwed up the courage to tell her the same thing last year. This was unfair. It had taken me a lot of planning and cool nonchalance to pull it off at all.

All during the day I'd see her sneaking little peeks at him, and he at her. You could have cut the sexual tension with a knife. Sue Ann was not exactly a vestal virgin, so the talk went, so I got to watching them to see where this would all lead. Since I lost them about lunch time, any guesses are pure conjecture.

I'll tell you, Pete and I were gossiping like a pair of old women. We couldn't wait to tell Harold and the rest of the guys when they saw fit to come back. We never got the chance—not Pete at least.

I got to know about Pete almost as soon as it happened. I guess his dad had relented and let him hunt on Thursday after all. The ambulance met the school bus—lights flashing. Pete only lived two farms away and my mother knew the whole story from listening in on the phone. One of Pete's uncles had shot a deer—only the deer was Pete. Mother said the ambulance was a waste of time. The uncle had a 30-06 and even if he couldn't hit a deer, he didn't miss poor Pete.

It was another of those stupid accidents that shouldn't happen. That's what my Dad said, and he handed us all blaze orange hats. He must have gone to town specially to get them. He didn't want to talk about it at all, but he kept looking at me, and finally said I could stay home Friday anyway, but be careful.

I was careful. So was Pete. A lot of good that had done him. I got to thinking about Terry. I wondered how he would take it. He had gone hunting on Thursday too. Would he still be in his talkative mood?

It was quite a bit into Monday before I paid any attention to Terry. There were lots of long faces around school anyway, so his didn't exactly stand out. He didn't seem any different than normal—his normal. When I tried to talk to him, I didn't get any more response than if I'd been talking to a jaded plough horse.

It was spring before I saw Terry in a jovial mood again. Spring in the townships meant working the land, cows calving, sheep lambing and football at school. Now our school was small, you may have gathered that; in order to have two football teams all the boys played. The little yappy grade niners, the long haired thirteens and of course us cool guys.

This is where Harold really shone. He was captain of one team, a playing captain. Coach was captain of the other, and I was on his team, alongside Terry. Damned old Harold was having a good time running over me at the line. The big son-of-a-bitch could just as easily run over one of the ginky five year crowd, but no. He was taking some kind of perverse pleasure in stampeding over me. It hurt. We had no protection of any kind. That's why it was flag football — everybody running around with a rag hanging out of his ass like a bunch of deranged white-tailed deer.

Harold was one hell of an athlete. He loved to win. I mean, he really loved it. If Harold had a weakness, it was his over-competitive nature. I have seen him cry real honest-to-God tears when he lost a game, even if it was just a silly all-the-school-on-two-sides flag football game. It was kind of embarrassing for those of us who knew him and looked up to him. The big crybaby.

Terry's brother was on Harold's team. The kid was a good athlete. Like Terry could have been. Harold had run over me one time too many, so I had ducked around the side and was covering their receivers. Terry's brother was in the clear. I could just about see the crosshairs of their quarterback on him, so I headed right at him — my eyes focused on his flag. He didn't catch the ball. There was something deliberate in the way he fumbled it, like he didn't want it. I glanced at his face; he wasn't even looking at me, or the ball which was bouncing around with a bunch of husky young farmers pursuing it. Instead, he was staring across the field. I followed his gaze and saw Terry — all smiles — waving at Sue Ann on the side lines. Coach came over and put his arm around Terry in that way he had. He said something. Terry laughed, his teeth shining, and ran down to the end of the line. His brother walked past me, and his face was pale. He saw me watching Terry and lifted one eyebrow. I noticed that he played really conservatively the rest of the game. I thought maybe I'd be careful, too.

Terry played as if possessed, making two touchdowns in a losing cause; but that all seemed irrelevant compared to the big blow-out I saw between Coach and the principal. I don't know what it was about. All I heard were some angry words, accompanied by a lot of finger waving and red faces. It must have been something important, because that night Coach hanged himself.

It could have been a coincidence, but I made a study of old Terry after that.

It happened twice the next year, the same cracking of Terry's shell, followed the next day or that night by somebody's death. Got so I dreaded seeing Terry in a happy mood. I didn't say anything to anybody else but I paid really close attention to Terry's mood swings, and if he looked likely to crack a smile, I was very cautious.

I don't know where Terry went after graduation. He moved away. I can picture him working on an

ambulance or maybe as a cop or something—maybe
a coroner. I don't want to know. If I never see his
smiling face again, that's fine with me.

Junkyard Dog

This is a true story, or at least I was told it was a true story. Which is just about all I can say about anything. Now it may be bullshit — I can guarantee that it is never going to be seen on "Cops" or "America's Funniest Police Videos." But it should be.

I know this guy, Duke. (The names have been changed to protect the admittedly guilty.) He was a kid down in the city. What city? I don't remember; it doesn't matter, they are all pretty much the same as near as I can see. You know, the downtown all hustle and bustle, the uptown all hills and fancy, and then there's the rest running from suburbia to the apartment houses and beyond.

Duke lived in beyond. He only wanted a few things in life, but he wanted them real bad — a car, sex, and a future, in that order. You see, the car was necessary for the other two to be possible. This story's about the car. Getting one was supposed to be easy — just steal it. The local gossip was always about that in his crowd, but the truth was that stealing a car was a short term and risky solution at best. You could buy a car, of course, but good paying jobs were rare, and they always needed money at home.

So Duke kinda split the difference. He bought a car, a sort of moldering motor-seized hulk, and set out to steal all the parts to fix it. In other words almost the entire car. See, Duke lived just down a back alley from a big scrap yard, so all he had to do was buy something fairly common, and fix it up. He got hold of some tools and got to studying that junkyard.

It had a high chain-link fence and gate, and a great big vicious German shepherd dog out at night. Every morning the grouchy old guy who owned the place would come and put food in the dog's kennel, and the dog would run in, and old grumpy would shut the door for the day. All day long this "King" shepherd — that's what they called those huge oversized dogs; I guess to differentiate them from shepherds of normal size and disposition — all day long he sat there and watched the people walk by. If they stopped close to him he growled, and they moved on nervously, or better still yelled at him to "Shut up!" with their voices pitched higher than normal, and tinged with fear. Nobody paid much attention to him other than that — the old man let him out at night, and cleaned the faeces out of the pen; in the morning he fed and watered him and shut the door. Even the owner's son and the other two guys who worked there steady didn't approach him. Because that's the way the owner wanted it. He usually got what he wanted.

Duke saw all this, and he started going to the junkyard, buying this or that, looking for what he previously had noted was not there. He even got a

little part time work, piling tires, batteries and crap.
Took the pile of dog shit from beside the kennel and
wheelbarrowed it away to the back where he covered
it with dirt. He was there most weekends. He didn't
fool with the dog, but he'd hum a little while shovelling
up the dog shit, the big shepherd just sitting and
watching him.

When the dog was out at night nobody in their right
mind would have tried to go inside that fence; Duke
never even saw the old man try that. When the old
man drove up in the morning, the dog would run stiff-
legged to the gate, his snarl just barely concealed by
his lips. Once he saw it was the old man, he'd trot back
over and sit down by the kennel door — not inside, it
made the old man nervous to be inside with him. He
fed the dog just after he opened the gate. He had a tap
and a covered garbage pail just inside, with a bunch
of five gallon buckets. He'd take one and fill it with
water, and while it was filling scoop a hubcap-full of
dry dog food into another hydraulic pail, and walk
toward the kennel. He'd refill the containers, walk past
the dog, and the dog would enter the kennel. Nothing
was said.

Duke saw all this. Now, Duke liked dogs, and
though he couldn't really have one of his own, he knew
the names of all the dogs he'd met, and even a couple
that he'd never been formally introduced to. As near
as Duke could ascertain, the junkyard dog did not
really have a name. Sometimes he was called the king
shepherd, and sometimes he was just called the dog,
or maybe, "my dog," as in "my wrench" or "my son,"
although Duke couldn't honestly say he'd ever heard
"my dog," just "the dog." So he started calling him

King. As in, "Do you want me to go shovel up King's shit now?" Or, "Jesus! It stinks over there; I think I should shovel out King every day."

Now it just so happened that there was a big butcher shop down the street a few blocks, always lots of scraps and trimmings. A lot of people shopped there, and nobody stopped him from rooting through the bin out back. If he talked to anybody he'd just say, "It's for my dog." Which was sort of the truth, although maybe it wasn't always believed, but that was okay too.

The first time he threw a juicy scrap of sirloin over the fence King didn't touch it at all. The next day Duke walked by with his shovel and his partly full five gallon bucket of dogshit, scooped up the morsel and buried it with the rest. He lingered beside the dog as he did so—"Hi King."

King growled of course; he growled at anything said to him, but Duke just hummed and went on his way to bury the shit. When he came back he leisurely floated the shovel with its smell of manure and ripe steak by the dog.

The next day he noted that King had dug up the buried steak, so that night he came back with a piece of round in a brown paper bag. When King heard someone approach the fence he barked once in warning and came wheeling around the corner of the garage. Duke was humming, "Hello King! Here you go." He threw the meat over by the sandy hillock where he buried the dog shit.

King gave him a hard look, but didn't snarl; he trotted over to the piece of meat, lying there smelling of blood and early decay. He licked his lips.

"Go ahead King! Good boy!"

King waited until Duke walked away, but he ate the steak.

Duke fed King every night—by Saturday when he was supposed to work at the junkyard the dog was taking the scraps out of his fingers through the fence. When he went to work, he waited until nobody was around before he buried the shit, which was just as well since King stuck out his tongue and even twitched his tail. The kid smiled and said, "Hi King!"

Before you could say "Turncoat," Duke had cut a careful hole through the fence and was shopping for car parts every second night. King stood watch. Duke didn't pet him or anything; he probably could have, but this was a business arrangement.

Of course the old man noticed this and that was missing. As near as Duke could figure the old fellow thought that his son was siphoning some off, but he couldn't prove it, because after all it wasn't true. Every night the old man would let that vicious dog out, and once or twice he even patrolled his fence looking for unlikely breaks. He didn't find any because Duke always carefully threaded a loose wire back into the two edges, making the gap hard to see—and hard to approach as well because it was on the pocked hillock where Duke buried the dog shit.

It went on like that for quite a while, and Duke could have got his old wreck on the road, if the old curmudgeon hadn't had a heart attack one Saturday as he was putting the big shepherd away. There he was down on the ground gasping away and trying to rise, with the damn dog standing guard over him. The son tried to approach, but King drove him back with snapping jaws. When Duke saw the commotion, the cruiser and the ambulance, they were all standing outside the closed gate.

"Shoot the Son-of-a-bitch!" said the son to the cop.

"I might hit the old man!"

The two ambulance attendants had their stretcher set up on the asphalt. "Well, we have to get in there immediately."

"Excuse me," said Duke, and he opened the gate. "Hi King!"

"Get to hell out of there!" said the son and the cop and several spectators.

Duke just walked along, humming. "Come on!" he beckoned to the dog as he filled the water, got some dog food and walked to the kennel. King followed him right inside and sat panting while the kid filled the containers. He shut the door.

"I should fire you," said the son, "but I imagine the old man will want to give you a promotion.

The Bull

Never trust a bull. It was one of the rules to live your life by. His father said it, and his grandfather repeated it. There were a whole bunch of rules applying specifically to bulls: don't pet the bull; if you have to hit a bull, hit him hard; do not try to handle a bull with a fork; don't walk between a bull and a wall; always consider a way of escape.

His mother had even drummed it home. "Look here!" she said. "It says here that more people are killed by domestic cattle worldwide than by all the lions and tigers and bears and everything else combined." She set the paper down—"You always be careful around the bull."

He had heard the horror stories, the neighbour whose father had been killed by a bull, way back when. "It took three shots with a .303 to get it off him. By then it was way too late."

"Way too late." He never pushed it, didn't ask the extent of the injuries. The thing is MacDonald still had to live with that memory, still had to keep a bull,

47

handle the bull, all the time, same as he and his father. They had to look into that big passive face and try to ascertain if violence and horrid death were lurking just under the surface. And yep, they were.

It was not that he had ever had any trouble with their bull. He leaned up against a pole in the hydro easement and studied George, their bull. George was named after the man that they had purchased him from, as were all their bulls. The big animal looked up passively, squinted at him, flapped his ears at some flies, and when spoken to went back to grazing among the rest of the herd. He was a Shorthorn (not that he had any horns at all), tawny red roan, supposed to be one of the worst breeds for undependability and sheer bad temper, but George looked harmless enough. The boy smiled to see that the big animal was here on one side of the herd and D4, a horned cow, was on the other side, with old B6 beside her. She was the boss cow, and the calves and weaker cows were safely bracketed between their protectors as they grazed the grass in the long slash through the bush that was the pole line.

The boy hitched his knapsack of fencing supplies up on his shoulder and walked past the cattle. "So Boss," he said, so as not to startle any that had not noticed him. Cattle in the bush were different than the same cattle in the barnyard or even in the open pasture field. The half-grown calves didn't just look at him as they would have normally, but scurried behind their mothers. He planned his route through the cattle so that he was on the far side of the pole line from George, but George seemed to pay no attention to him. He was studying the bush on the other side. There seemed something a bit aggressive in his stance, and afterward the boy wished he'd paid more attention to that, that and the way the cattle had sort of crowded together and around him as he went through.

Checking fence was a job he liked. Oh, there were always some mosquitoes, blackflies and deer flies but he had long ago learned that worrying about bugs was actually worse than the bugs.

His father and grandfather were haying, cutting in the morning and baling all day in the heat. There was no tractor left for him, and anyway his expertise in such matters was not yet fully developed, so when his dad had suggested that he check the back fence, he had been glad to do so.

"Mind the bull!" his grandfather had said as he helped the boy fill the knapsack with staples, wire cutters, insulators, fencing tool and machete for the brush by the electric fence. "Here, let me sharp that for you." The old man took a heavy stone and rhythmically wiped it against the blade. "They're no good unless they're sharp. Don't cut yourself."

The boy was downwind of the cattle now. He could smell the rich, sweet smell of them — and of the crushed grass they were grazing on. He hurried past. The cattle had their own personal retinue of biting insects. He climbed a little rise and came to where the electric fence cut through the pole line. It was fine, taut and straight. He took out his machete and cut some grass that was touching it. He stopped to study a pile of bear shit on the top of the ridge. It was full of green chokecherries. "I guess he couldn't make it to the road." The boy smiled. His father always joked about bears hurrying out of the bush with their legs cramped together so they could shit on the road. His father thought it was one of the ways they marked territory.

He followed the fence into the cool of the bush. There were more flies here but they were not overwhelming. Occasionally he adjusted an insulator. Once he replaced a missing one and pulled the snapping wire away from the metal post. The fence dipped down off the ridge toward the lake. He could smell the water, feel its coolness, and about the time he could see the opening in the tree tops that marked its presence, he came to a grand failure in the fence. Insulators were all gone, posts were pulled out and the wire up ahead was in a tangled ball. Black hair was mixed in the mess of wire and insulators. "Stupid bear!" said the boy, but he smiled to think of the squalling that must have erupted in this spot as the bear fought against the invisible stinging of the wire. It took him some time to untangle the mess. He had wire stretched here and there up and down the line. A considerable piece was missing, so it was lucky that he had brought a small roll with him for such a situation. "Stupid bear!"

He got the wire connected again, but even with the insulators he had with him and those he had managed to find in the mess, he hadn't enough to finish putting the fence up right. It would do for now, because by the sign, he could tell that the cattle seldom came over into this corner of the bush pasture. There wasn't much grass, and maybe they didn't like the presence of the bear. He decided that he might as well go for more insulators, and while he was at it, he thought maybe he would pick up his 30-30. Not that he was afraid of bears really, just that it was somewhat consoling to have a rifle along if you met one. They had lost a calf last summer and his father thought the bear was the culprit. What a coup it would be if he shot the bear!

He cut through on the old lake road that ran out to where the cattle were; there was no sense in backtracking along the fence. But this route would bring him sidewind of the cattle. He would need to sing out when he got close. He didn't much like the alert way that George had been gazing at the brush on this side. He wouldn't want to be mistaken for something he wasn't.

The boy stopped dead. In the mud of the old tractor road was a bear track, a very big bear track, a fresh big bear track. A cold thrill played with the hair on the back of his neck. Now he knew why George was so concerned with the bush on this side. The bear had been here very recently. Muddy water still swirled in the track. He thought he could smell the rank presence of the bear. "My mind playing tricks with me," he said loudly. "Ho! Mr. Bear, I'm a man. Bugger off!"

He took his machete out of the bag and freed it from its scabbard. He was painfully aware that the long knife was not a weapon but a tool. Its point was not even sharp. It would be poor protection from a bear, but he tried to reassure himself that the bear was not going to bother him anyway. The sharp edge of the machete was heartening. Big deal! He would get one slash! A lot of good that would do! "You're not going to bother me anyway, are you bear?"

"Woof!" said the bear.

The boy still couldn't see the bear, but he heard him plain enough now. The bear was deliberately breaking brush just beside him. The boy retreated down the tractor road toward the pole line. He tried to sound gruff. "If you are trying to scare me away from here, it's working, so bugger off!" His voice sounded a bit more hysterical and high pitched than he would have liked.

He looked back... Dammit! The bear was on the road behind him. He seemed perfectly business-like about the thing, did the bear. He sort of swayed from side to side as he came stalking down the road, his little back eyes gleaming nastily and his pigeon-toed feet getting him closer all the time.

"Bear! You get back!" said the boy. He wanted to run, but he knew that would be fatal. He had to win the bluffing contest. He made himself as big as he could. He waved his machete. "Fuck off, you black piece of shit!"

The bear took two more steps and stopped. He said something. The boy couldn't speak bear, but he knew that it was about how the boy was one hundred and thirty pounds of protein. Then the bear came on again. There was no bluff in this. The boy knew he was being hunted. He backed down the road, all the time waving the silly machete. He did the mental math. There was no way that the bear was not going to catch him — it was gaining steadily. Oh, if the boy acted really aggressive the bear would stop, but he always started on again, always closing the gap between them. The boy scooped up a fist-sized rock and threw it at the bear. He didn't bother trying to save his shoulder, but put everything into the throw. It thumped off the bear's back. The bear growled and hopped sideways, but then hopped even closer to him.

The damn thing was only a few metres away now. The boy wondered what it would feel like being eaten by a bear. He thought maybe he was going to piss his pants. He felt like crying—but he wouldn't give the son-of-a-bitch the satisfaction. He planned on cutting the bear across the face. It probably wouldn't stop him, but when they hunted him down later, they'd know they got the right bear and they'd know he died fighting.

He opened his mouth to shout at the bear, and then he thought of George, also not much more than a few metres away now—George who he'd been chopping all spring in the barnyard before he was turned out with the cows. "Co Boss, Co Boss, Co, Co!"

The bear stopped at this new loud call, then sort of shrugged and proceeded down the trail the last few metres to the boy. "Boss, Boss, Co Boss!" shouted the Boy.

Co Boss came—all twenty-three hundred pounds of him, thumping up the tractor road with an inquisitive bawl and three cows close behind. When George smelled the bear he bawled and slobbered— his great tongue lolling out of his mouth. He tore up a great clod of earth with his spade-like front foot and tossed it over his shoulder. His tail arched up over his back.

"Bear," said the boy, "I'd like you to meet my buddy, George."

The bear didn't want anything to do with George, or with his harem crowding the road behind him. But the bear had other problems because D4 and B6 had cut straight through the bush, thinking no doubt to beat the others to the chop they thought the boy had for them. Now they crashed through the spruce brush from the right almost on top of the bear, who roared and turned to meet this new threat. The cows' nostrils were suddenly full of his stench — the old lead cow and D4 with her sweeping Hereford horns were all that stood between the bear and their following calves. They roared and were on him like Nordic Goddesses.

The bear whirled to run and was hoisted by D4 and trod on by big B6. George may have been bluffing, but when the cows hit the bear, the bull responded immediately. He brushed by the boy, bounded in two thundering leaps to the bear and crashed onto him, his two front hooves driving him into the ground. The bear snapped at him on the way by but only grazed the muscled side. George had run over the bear. Now he turned with a shower of dirt and uprooted hazel gads. He bellowed and his eyes were rolling madness. The cows had backed off and they, the boy and the cattle behind him, stood and roared and hollered for George to crush the bear. George charged in little hops. His neck and head and nose struck out in fast thrusts until the roaring snapping bear was lifted and thrown against a big spruce. As it bounced back off the tree, the bear gamely turned in the air and was on George's neck. George erupted into the air, his huge head flailing and his hindquarters bucking. The bear slipped down the side leaving bloody tears, and George shouldered him into the base of the tree. The boy could hear ribs and the lower branches of the spruce shattering together. George snorted and roared, backed off half a length and then threw his mass against the bear again. His giant front hoof pawed and trampled the screaming bear out from under the tree and the bull leapt on him, pounding him with his front feet. By now, the slobber was flying two metres from the corners of his mouth and the filament of his fury hung around his head like a veil.

The bear was dead but George wasn't through with him. The boy said later that he thought maybe George wanted to kill the bear's ancestors clean back to before man. When he finally stopped and the cows had taken turns trampling the carcass, they stood around him and snuffled the bull's wounds and cheered his victory. And the bull had looked at the boy finally. The slime was drying on George's sides, the blood was still seeping from his wounds and the bear's blood was on his legs and on his shoulders and on his great triumphant head. The bull looked across centuries to the boy.

The boy looked back. He grinned, then thought better of that. Showing his teeth didn't seem like a good idea.

George turned his head and looked at the wreckage of the bear, and the uprooted trees and torn duff. The boy was just on the other side of this new clearing. The bull arched his great muscled neck and turned his head back to the boy.

The boy turned and walked away. "Never trust a bull," he said.

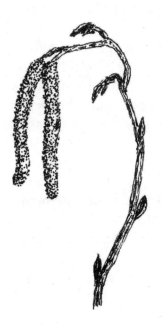

The Fox

The fox was lying on a dry bit of sand. It was warm; the sun was shining down on him, but he was the same color as the sand, as best he could see. And he could see pretty well.

All down below him was a giant lacework of sugar maples. Of course he didn't think of them as sugar maples, just as beautiful, and as allowing a view of half the world from his sandy, sunny spot. He could see a long way out through the maples. Snowshoes came out into them, eating the little red gads that grew in low bunches here and there among the trees. A bad spot to be a rabbit in. He smiled and thought about a rabbit.

A rabbit! Where was that rabbit? He was behind him, that's why he thought of that snow-bouncing, squealing, succulent, snowshoe hare. The rabbit was in the thick tangle of dogwood up behind him. That was the fox's escape route, into the wind, through the snarl of little dogwoods, the biggest the size of his leg — nothing could catch him in those dogwoods. Three

57

young coyotes tried once; his heart pounded, and the world got really concentrated, but he outmaneuvered them easily, broke through onto the burn, and toyed with them. Out in the good going, with nobody to cut him off, he could tease them — had they not been young coyotes they would have been too smart to chase him out in the open.

He grinned to think of that, but it was a pained grin, and his tongue lolled out. Why was he thinking about coyotes?

Coyote! Oh, it was just the whiff, where the male coyote had marked. They traveled along this ridge, but seeing how the wind was seeping off the flat above and wandering down into the maple valley below, the coyotes couldn't sneak up on him. Not that they bothered trying, especially when there were lots of snowshoes, and the men were hunting again.

Men! Where were men? Oh, a truck was driving up the blind line down to the south of him. This was a common thing in the fall. The men were hunting. That was good; they didn't hunt him. They didn't even try to trap him anymore, hadn't for two winters. It was a good time to be a fox.

Boy, no other fox had better be on his territory!

That little female from south of the road had come over into those maples a few times. He tolerated that, not minding that their ranges overlapped a bit — looking forward to winter. He grinned and stretched on the sand.

Then he sat up. Of course there was that young male from a litter born down in the big cedar swamp, on the other side of the next burn. The very north end of his range, where the old bitch was. He smirked. That pup better not think he could carve out some territory here!

Why was he thinking of foxes? The faint whiff left by the coyote was nothing like fox. One thing a fox like him could do was mark territory. He scoffed at the pitiful effort of the coyotes, or the even more feeble trace left by the little dog down by the farm.

No, it wasn't the dog from the farm. He didn't run out this far anyway.

Something was moving at the very periphery of vision, way down through the maples. Something red. It was far away, down where the water lay, down where the tag alders grew, at the very centre and mouth of the little valley. It wasn't a fox. It was the wrong colour of red. It was a Man! He was a long way away though, way down through the shining maples. Men didn't shoot at him lately. Still, he didn't give them a chance when they were hunting. But they only hunted sometimes. Mostly in these few days in the late fall. He'd seen it four times. He was a wise old dog fox.

This man was making lots of noise. It wasn't just that he was breaking ice, the big clumsy dolt, but he was pushing brush out of his way, trampling some under. It was a wonder the poor foolish thing was moving upwind!

Wait...now he wasn't; the stupid creature had turned and was wandering down the valley with the wind. The fox grimaced in contempt. That man wasn't likely to see a deer, let alone kill it. They killed a lot of deer though. Deer are too big anyway, but if a man kills one, he leaves all the best stuff. The blood, the guts. Men, blood, deer guts.

Now what was that man doing? He was scrambling up the fox's side of the valley; the fox heard him and smelled him at the same time. What kind of hunting was that? Men move like cows, only faster, and more in a straight line. But this man was going in a pattern like a hunter, zig zagging, but he was so noisy and so stupid, and traveling downwind half the time...peuh! —men can really mark territory.

The man was urinating. The fox didn't care. He could share range with a man; they were no competition.

By the smell of things, this one had killed a deer yesterday, and a fawn. Just like a stupid fawn to get shot by a clumsy idiot. The fox turned his face away from the human and scanned the maples for something to eat, or something dangerous.

What had he seen? Something had moved down in the maples at the edge of his vision, just a jot of movement, but fairly low down, not a bird. Maybe a snowshoe! Did he dare go running around after a snowshoe with a man hunting right beside him? No. He wasn't hungry anyway. He had fed on a pile of guts over on the next burn, at the end by the pond; not the deer this man had shot. A buck. The guy he had seen sitting by the poplar narrows must have shot him. Same smell was around the deer. That same smoking stuff, with the bitter taste when it's out.

The clumsy man was burning some of that weed now. He coughed, loud as a cow. Oh, watch out deer! The fox grinned and pushed the sand with his nose.

There it is! Ah...the thing in the maples was plain to see now, just a woodpecker, a downy, looking for grubs under the bark. TapTapTap...taptap. Naw, there was nothing much there. The bird flew a bit closer. The fox lazily watched him

The man was moving again, struggling through the dogwoods on top of the ridge. Why didn't he just go northeast a bit out onto the prairie? The gun could kill a long way, but nothing was going to let him walk up close enough to see, not in those dogwoods. Of course there hadn't been any deer here since last night, and they were just traveling through. Two bucks, and both of them in rut, a traveling show that. The largest of them had been fairly big, with a full set of antlers, strong! You could still smell where he passed. The younger buck had lagged behind. No telling what he thought he was going to gain out of it. Looking for a doe maybe, if the big buck got into a fight with another alpha male. The fox had seen it happen.

Now the man was heading back to the maple valley again, crashing right through the dogwoods. What a fool! The fox stood up, unsure what the man was doing. He didn't seem like much of a threat, but had been around on three sides of him now. It made the fox nervous. He stuck his tongue out, tasted the air, glanced slant-eyed in the direction of the scent...then panted and lay back down. He was safe here; the man was swishing down the side of the maples, through the leaves — was now coming into view.

Just peering over the edge of the eroded sandbank, the fox was nearly invisible, and he knew it. Curiously he watched the man, listened to his sounds, and smelled him.

The whiffs of the man's breakfast smelled wonderful. There had been some of that meat those men make; he had tasted it, put out for the little dog.

At night, scraps—they burned meat...fire.

The man was lighting another smoking thing. They burned that weed. He had seen them burn trees too. Once the farmer, clearing off a corner. And once a bunch of humans, young ones he thought. At night, and he had looked at the fire closely; they were silly, and were making noises like a flock of geese in a field.

A V of geese was going by, way up high, a last flock leaving—too bad. He couldn't see them but they were calling to each other. Of course humans made all kinds of noises.

The man was sitting down on a maple log. He spoke! Sort of a mutter, but definitely spoken. Usually they did that together, even when they were obviously hunting. They spoke a lot. Sometimes they howled and hollered; they were driving deer then. Coyotes tried the same thing with snowshoes; he'd seen the brush wolves do it with deer.

That man sure smelled like a deer. Oh, what's this! He was rustling around now, funny sound of rustling, and smell of food. Maybe the man was going to leave some scraps! Yup, he did! The fox saw the man throw the stuff, arching down the ridge. There was something shiny, that skin-like stuff, not good to eat. But something heavier hit too. That was scrap. The fox would trot over and eat it as soon as the man was gone, and before a whiskyjack came along and took it.

He could hear a whiskyjack now, off to the south. Those damn things, you couldn't catch them, and they would steel you blind; they even followed the men along. So did ravens, though not so close.

There was a raven. The fox could just see the black speck patrolling the edge of the far burn. He was not any more likely to let the man have a shot at him than the fox was. If that whiskyjack stayed where he was the fox was definately going to eat the scraps the man had tossed away. He had eaten this before, lots of time; some funny stuff people eat. All good though. Strange creature, man, nothing else like him. Dogs were like wolves, like foxes, like coyotes. Deer were like cattle, and kind of like horses. Men were like nothing else. The unfathomable stuff they did!

The man was moving again, side-hill along the edge of the ridge, skidding occasionally — a deer might think he was a cow; there were still cows in the range. He could hear some bawling in the distance. Tractor... the man who lived here was feeding the cows. There was hay on the ground where the cows ate, mice sometimes, afterbirth in the spring.

The clumsy man was out of sight, but he still smelled strong. Men sometimes smell strong, sometimes they don't smell at all. The fox had smelled one once with the odour of a fox on him. It had nearly fooled the fox, so it could easily fool a deer. Men are strange things. They have a hot smell, with a deep musk to it, and of course they smelled a bit like their scat; everything smells a bit like its scat.

That was cow shit he was smelling now, fresh; couldn't smell the cow...a long way, this carried a long way. The man is a long way, out of sight; even if the fox were to go as far as he could see, the man was farther than that. The fox got up, stretched, looked around just in case, and trotted angleways down the ridge, straight to the scraps the man had left. He nosed aside the skin-like shiny stuff, and ate the scraps. They were good, exotic, with a funny texture.

Might as well follow. It would be easy to stay out of sight of this man, and his gun.

The fox didn't follow right on the man's footprints, but up on the edge of the ridge, in the dogwoods. He peered out once in a while, out over the mouth of the valley; the man wasn't down there. There was a movement in a bunch of pine growing on the last shoulder of the ridge; something was over there traveling through the pines, out toward the burn. It was the man—he had a certain cadence, steady, yet clumsy. And he thumped the toe of his big, funny man feet on the ground now and then, as if he could hardly pick up his feet. Bucks walked like that sometimes, so did cattle. This was a male, most men were males; there were females, but he had seldom seen them.

The fox cut through the band of dogwoods, dip, dip, dip, across some standing water, and to the burn edge, where he stopped, sat down and studied the burn. The man should come out over where the pine were on the edge, down past where a tumble of boulder thrust up through the flat rock, past a decaying bunch of poplars forlornly trying to grow in the burn. Down along the gaddy edge. There he was.

The fox was nearly sure the man would go the other way, down to the end of the burn, or maybe across it, but no, the man headed up toward the fox. The fox was nervous. Why was he coming this way, was he hunting the fox?

No! He wasn't hunting at all. True, he had the gun in his hand, and men are strange things. But he was walking right up the centre of the burn. Now he was running! The fox grimaced.

He was definately running, slow—clomp, clomp,

clomp. He was making a funny noise, sort of like panting, sort of like pups in a den. He hollered, then he spoke, very loud; he hollered again, much like a calf separated from its mother. He was probably trying to contact another human.

Like a coyote. Well, not like a coyote; the man had turned around in the burn. He jerked the gun up and shot. The smash of the report hurt the fox's ears, echoing off the forest edging the burn. The man had stopped again; he stood for a moment in the middle of the burn, then started walking steadily down the centre, south past the fox.

The man must be going to the road—he had come from the road; he was associated with the truck that had gone by earlier. Men are in trucks. There is nothing like a man.

But what was this strange man doing now? Here he was heading back into the dogwoods down south on the other side of the fox, a place he had been just a little while ago. Did he think something was following him? Was that why he was cutting back on his trail? The fox smiled. Something was following him—a stealthy fox.

Crash! The fox skittered sideways. But it was only the man again. He must have fallen in the dogwoods. He spoke again, then hollered—no other man answered him. What was he up to?

The fox ducked his head and traversed the length of the band of dogwoods. When he got to where the man had walked he followed the ragged track and came again to the edge of the ridge, not far south of where the man had climbed. As the fox blinked in puzzlement, the man puffed along on the edge of the ridge, slipped, bounced off a maple, spoke, and slid down the side-hill, until he came to the fallen maple he'd sat on a while before, when he'd left the scraps.

The man sighed like a dying rabbit and sat down on the log. The fox thought that he might as well be comfortable so he slipped along the edge of the ridge, back to his little sandy ledge, settled in and watched the man.

The man hollered. He spoke. He took out some of that burning leaf, and the acrid, hot smell came to the fox's nose. He coughed, loud again, like a cow. He was looking around now, the fox could see his head swivel. He stopped, then bent over, looking at the shiny stuff that had wrapped the scraps. He spoke again, stood up, turned around. He put his hands to his face and made a noise like pups in a den.

Why was the man doing that? If he were not such a frightening alien thing he would attract a predator. The fox had seen a man once in the winter making a sound sort of like a dying rabbit. Not quite, but sort of. He had seen that, and he had been amazed all over again about men.

This man stood, hollered again, and set out back across the little valley, down through the maples, up the other side. The fox could still see flashes of his coat, and twice the man hollered.

The fox yawned and stretched out on the sand. Who knew what the man was doing? But he was gone now. The fox didn't understand men. Men were the most interesting things.

After a while the sun had warmed the valley, and the air had begun to flow over the fox. It was time to move; it did not pay to lie with downwind out of sight.

Simply because he wanted to travel into the wind the fox trotted down through the maples to check in the tag alders by the mouth of the little valley. Snowshoes had been there, but they were gone since early morning. The fox had no intention of going very far. Not with the bush full of men. Men!

He tilted his head sideways and swiveled his ears; yes, that was the cadence of a man moving, heading north on the other side of the tag alders—the same goofy man from before.

The fox had an idea; he licked his lips as he thought of it. That man must be flushing game ahead of him all the time. If he were to jump a snowshoe, it wouldn't run out into the open wet burn on the other side of the man—no, it would head toward the fox. The fox had done this before with a big old timber wolf that was hunting deer. He would travel parallel to the man, in the spruce.

It worked too; the fox had hardly started shadowing along just out of sight of the man when a young snowshoe came boiling through the low spruce. The thrill of the hunt was in the fox; his vision was locked on the rabbit; one-two leaps and he was in front of it. It dodged, snowshoes are good at that, but the fox was onto the trick, and he swiveled with the snowshoe. He was only two jumps behind, keeping his eyes on the ears—snowshoes always flatten their ears before they dodge. As soon as the bunny moved his ears, the fox cut hard left and the snowshoe ran right into him. It rolled its eyes as he caught it; it had no time to squeal. It is best if they don't squeal; the squeal can give a hunter away. The blood filling his mouth, he carried his rabbit under the spreading branches of a spruce to eat it, starting with the guts.

Once finished he felt sleepy, but it was not wise to sleep where you have eaten, too much scent around. There was a thick patch of juniper out in the long prairie nearby; it was a good place to sleep, sheltered and yet offering a panoramic view. He would go there.

He followed a cattle trail. Cattle make deep, smooth trails, very quiet walking, and they join up places nicely. There were cattle nearby, one had walked down this trail only a few moments before, and it was probably going to the burn too. No, there it was standing beside a clump of poplars. The cow was looking north, and the fox followed her gaze, into the eyes of the big buck from the morning, looking right at him. The fox smiled — the smart old deer had heard him, quiet as the shadow of a feather, stealthy silent on the cattle trail. And that noisy man thought he could catch the deer. Ha!

Good hearing or not, the big buck was silly with the rut. He even shook his massive antlers at the fox, although he knew damn well it was a fox. The fox bounded stiff-legged toward the deer, who stamped his hoof and shook his head vigorously, raking a nearby shrub and grunting. The fox waggled his head, then flipping his tail scampered out toward the clearing.

He stopped when he came to the edge of the long burn. What was he doing traveling around in the open in broad daylight? There could be men anywhere.

There had been a man here! Not the silly one, but the one that had killed the buck down at the other end of the burn. He was nowhere in sight, but he had traveled along the edge of the burn not too long ago.

The fox sat perfectly still and studied the burn. A point on a bit of a ridge came out to his right where the deer crossed. The fox could see his bunch of junipers out in the burn directly in front of him. He started out...and knew he was being watched. His head swiveled side to side.

A whistle! Like a birdcall — but not a birdcall — from the ridge where the deer cross. The fox's eyes narrowed. He could see nothing there. He stopped and concentrated on the point. Nothing. He started on again; the whistle sounded again. His head swiveled sideways, and he turned and slunk back to the protection of the bush line. There was no doubt the man was somewhere in those trees. The fox could not see the man, but the man had seen the fox — it made his blood run cold. He would not go out in the open again in daylight, not until the snow came and the men were gone.

The fox had to know exactly where the man was; there was a lesson to be learned in it. He turned to his right and travelled inside the edge of the bush to where he knew the wind from the point had to be blowing in. He could smell no man. Raccoon! Yes, a raccoon on the ridge...but it wasn't a raccoon that he had smelled before; there was a sort of aftertaste to it. He lifted his head and inhaled deeply, the air washing over the folded wonder of his inner nose. Yes, this was not a raccoon; this was a man pretending to be a raccoon, just like the one before had tried to smell like a fox. Men were wonderful, and dangerous.

The fox lay down where he was, in a little bunch of dead grass, saw grass, sharp. He clicked his front teeth together thoughtfully. This was a dangerous place —

if anything came up behind him, traveling into the wind, he wouldn't smell it, and the cow trail was so quiet he might not hear it. His only good line of escape was out past the man on the ridge. Yes, he was sure there was a man on the ridge, although evidence was scarce. He did not want to travel back down the trail, downwind. He looked to his right, further along this edge of the burn. Through the poplars, birch and spruce there was a cedar point that had snowshoes sometimes, and roughed grouse usually. Now it was a safe place. He would go sidewind there.

The fox hoped he wouldn't run into the big dog fox that had his range in the cedar point. He would be poaching in the other fox's territory — there had been a nasty confrontation the last time. He had made a territory mark on a clump of grass, and the other fox had chased him well back into his own area before going home. Now he felt nervous even well within his own boundary. He showed his teeth, but his tail drooped; he did not want to run into that other dog fox, not here, especially not here in his own territory. Then he would have to fight. He couldn't give up the edge of the burn and his favourite bunch of junipers out in the centre. He would fight! Was that him?

No, it was the big buck; the shadows were starting to stretch out into the burn and the deer was out patrolling his rubs. Even in full rut he moved quietly. He stopped, smelling the fox, arched his neck at the scent, and looked out into the open of the burn. The fox sat quietly on his haunches and watched.

The big buck walked stiff-legged past him, out into the edge of the burn where he had a scrape beside a scrubby little maple. He pawed dirt off it, freshing it

up, and urinated in it, then carefully stepped right in
the centre, leaving his big track there. He rubbed the
gland on his nose against an overhanging branch,
licked the branch, and rubbed his nose again. The hair
was standing up on his back — another buck must have
been at the scrape. He glared at the fox, as if somehow
he was responsible. The fox reacted to his attitude and
left his own whiff on some red gads.

The buck stepped out of his rub, arching his neck
back and scratching his back with the tip of one of his
long antler tines. Then he snuffled the ground. The
fox could see and smell that the deer had caught the
scent of a doe that had passed lately, though its exact
location was in doubt. The buck lifted his great head
and tasted the air, curling his lip back, showing his
gums. He lowered his head and went out into the open,
his nose close to the ground.

When the fox heard the whistle he knew what it
was, but the buck didn't; it stopped and glared over
toward the point — where the man was. The fox heard
the bullet hit the deer before he heard the shot. The
big buck took one jump and fell; he thrashed once and
was still. The fox could smell the blood. This was good
for him; he backed a bit further into the bush and
waited.

The man was climbing out of a tree; the fox could
see him clearly now. He had never seen one up in a
tree before; he would think of that next time, yes he
would. The man walked over to the deer; he spoke
quietly, and lit one of the smoking things, a bigger,
sweeter smelling one. The man spoke again and the
fox realized he was looking at him. He didn't run; the
man showed his teeth. The fox sat stock still and

watched while he gutted the deer, tossing the liver toward the fox. He spoke again and showed his teeth; there was no threat in it.

When the man walked away out into the burn, the fox approached the liver; it didn't pay to wait too long, and a raven was already circling around. The fox heard a commotion: the clumsy man he had seen earlier was clomping down the burn, shouting at the man who had shot the deer, running toward him waving his arms. They spoke together, the clumsy one noisily. Soon they turned back toward the dead deer, still gabbling away together. Somehow they pulled the big buck up into a little maple, and left him there partly off the ground.

The fox retreated with a piece of the liver and watched them from just inside the bush. The deer killer didn't seem to wish him any harm, as if he knew that the fox, and the raven for that matter, were more interested in the guts than the carcass of the deer. The deer killer spoke, and then the clumsy man looked over and saw the fox. He lifted his gun but the deer killer spoke loudly; the clumsy one put his gun on his back and they walked away.

The fox sat with one foot on his piece of liver; it was soft and warm under his foot, and its odour was enticing, but he didn't want to take his eyes off the men. Before they walked around the point the deer killer looked back at the fox and grinned — there was no doubt it was a grin.

The fox grinned back.

Long Lake

W e were paddling up moose hunting, already a day and a half in on the old canoe route. We had killed one moose, expressed it out to the truck, the long drive and the cooler. Had nearly got another that morning but we screwed it up. Not an uncommon occurrence when calling moose.

I had also got into quite an argument with an outfitter — my canoe and his boat mutually held together while we yelled in each other's faces. He had bunches of hunters on every lake.

"Where are you going to go now?" he growled.

I told him, but he didn't like it. "I got a crew on Frying Pan, and another on Five Star. Don't go through there! And don't stay here either; I got a big crew on this lake!"

I explained how this was a century old canoe route through Crown Land and me and my three buddies could damn well go where I wanted to.

He had made a few suggestions as to where I could go, and he spoke of things like livelihood and business

73

while I spoke of things like sovereignty and freedom, and though we never came to blows it was close. It ended amiably enough with a compromise where he'd pull us down the long skinny lake with his motorboat and we'd going up Sauble which he seemed willing to surrender to us damn locals.

See the truth was that if he had bunches of bumbling tourists on every lake on the interior route I didn't want to go through there anyway. Besides we had already shot or frightened off the local bulls.

My plan was to camp the night on Boumage and spend a day or so there before wandering over to Bark. I had fought and cajoled and nagged the guys so that we could make any portage in three trips: Trip one—four men: rifles, personal packs, one rifle carried back. Trip two—two men on food packs, one man kitchen pack, one man tent pack. Trip three—two men on two canoes, two men on booze packs.

Of course if we were dragging a moose along with us it took at least another trip. Still, that wasn't bad and it meant that we could do one of the normal two smoke portages in part of a morning and still put a lot of distance down on the map, cruising along through moose country, stopping to glass the swamps, calling long and horny out into the ridges following the lakes. It wasn't a hardship, regardless of what most of the rest of them thought. Not for young men on a warm fall with lots of rutting bulls in the bush.

We'd camp with the fire crackling and no other light; we'd wash the blood off our hands and we'd sing songs of times long ago, when we first came to this land, and songs of the old country, about being in the highlands, about the dark islands, songs of death and sorrow, night songs. We would sit and drink rum and coffee by the fire. We told lies; things look different when remembered by a fire. It does something to a man—farmers change in the darkness, the blood sort of seeps in them; clerks and office men crack their knuckles in the direct heat of flames; the wind at night whispers in schoolteachers' ears. It changes men to be back where we are supposed to be.

It was the first trip up into this country for my buddies. They had all canoed before except one, and he was a fast learner, so it was good, all of us good hunters, safe and old friends. We didn't even complain or whine when it started to rain that day, although it got less cheerful all the time. "To hell with Boumage," I said. "Long Lake will do just as well!"

There was no complaint about that. We put the canoes in the corner of Long and headed up for a sheltered cove that looked good on the map. It wasn't a spot I'd ever camped before because I had always come through in the spring or summer fishing; the weather was a little meaner now and flies no problem. Narrows were what we were looking for, funnels to squeeze the moose crossings down.

We came around the second corner of Long, and our projected campsite was in view. On a little summer camp island was a bunch of guys; two or three big prospector tents were on the island's bare crest behind them. "Shit!" I said.

The men gathered down by the water's edge in a sullen group, about thirty or forty metres in from the broadside of my canoe. We waved and continued paddling past; no one waved back, they spoke excitedly back and forth, then one whistled loud and shrill through his teeth. "Hey! Where do you think you're going?"

"We are going to make camp out of the wind." I pointed ahead.

The guy on shore squared his shoulders and glanced at his buddies. "This lake is taken!"

"Taken?" I questioned.

"Yah!" said another of them. "It's ours."

"Oh." I lay my paddle across the gunwales. "Do you have a deed?"

The first that spoke sort of puffed himself up. "Did you check with anybody before you came in here?"

I rolled a smoke. "I don't have to check with anybody. This is crown land!"

"You didn't check with an outfitter?" He shook his head. "Well you will just have to fuck off. Where did you think you were going anyway?"

"I don't have to check with an outfitter; this is an old established canoe route. My Grandfather used this canoe route you kitchimookmaan son-of-a-bitch."

"Fuck you!" he said. "You might as well turn around because the outfitter that flew us in has guys on every lake from here in. How the hell did you get up here anyway?"

"You're on a canoe route!" I said to him. "Are you stupid?"

"Come to shore; I'll show you who is stupid!"

I was just about to do just that. Okay, there were eight or nine of them, but if the speaker was their big man, they didn't impress me much. They were not big men, shorter than us mostly, and carrying less weight as an average and not as muscley. Besides I knew my boys were mean and warmed up; a good fight might be just the thing. Anyway I'd had enough of his God-damned lip, and told him so.

I was on the point of picking up my paddle when I saw the bowman in my canoe move his right arm back a bit. You know how it is, if you travel with someone, canoe with him, tent, talk, hunt and drink long into the night year after year, it gets so that you don't have to speak to read him. My bowman was a quiet man, not pretentious, not loud—I paid attention to him. And now when his arm moved like that I followed it down to the hand, and saw the hand go around the pistol grip of his rifle, hold the safety back so that it made no click, and slide it off. I looked over at my other two buddies, behind us and a bit farther from the island, and saw that they were drifting broadside, saw that they had back paddled for an uninterrupted field of fire and were kneeling on the floor, their asses braced across the seat thwarts and each had his rifle held across his thighs.

"I don't want to fight!" I said to the guy on the shore. "This is ridiculous. I'll be reporting this to the game warden, but I don't want to fight, there is no need for this!" I felt like I was just teetering on the edge of a cliff with my arms flailing; events were about to get away from me, and I wasn't sure I could stop the slide. I looked down at my rifle lying against a pack in front of me. I had already shot a moose so the sling was closed over a thwart; the clip was in it though nothing was in the chamber. I visualized myself unsnapping the quick swivel, levering a round into the chamber and opening fire. I would have to open fire if my buddies did. Scanning quickly, I could see no rifles in the hands of the men on shore; they must be up at the camp.

"Come on," said the guy on shore, "just you and me!"

"No," I said. "I'd love to, but not with everybody carrying a rifle."

"Don't worry about that!" He seemed oblivious to the certain death sitting in front of him.

"Well," I picked up my paddle, "we are going now. Everyone's got a knife on his belt, we all have rifles somewhere, and I don't need this." I waved at my buddies who seemed almost reluctant to put down their rifles.

"Next year," shouted the fool on the shore, "check with an outfitter before you go somewhere."

We paddled back to the portage; the sternman in the other canoe said softly, "I thought we were going to have to shoot them." He had not said anything to the man on shore, none of them had, all they had done was prepare to shoot.

I pointed out that that was insane, that you can't just open fire on men. "I thought you were going to get us all killed!"

"Well," he said, "we knew how crazy you were!"

"How crazy I am!" I growled. "You were going to start shooting men."

"It was us or them!" said his bowman.

We argued like that all the way to the portage. As we were pulling the canoes up, gear and all, onto the high bank, we heard an outboard coming. "It's them!" My buddies reached for their rifles. "Now we are on shore!"

"Unload those God-damned rifles!" I said. They were stubborn; the Woodsman canoe with two men and a kicker came around the corner. "Unload them, let him see you do that!"

"But what if they open fire?" I explained that they weren't going to open fire, but that if someone had to have a loaded rifle it would be me, and I slung my rifle under my arm. I stepped closer to the water and nodded at the older men in the canoe. They never landed but floated to a halt just off our bank. "That was a tense situation back there wasn't it?" said the guy in the bow.

"It certainly was!"

"Those guys are just greenhorns; I flew them in. They didn't even have a gun on them; I make them store them unloaded up by the camp."

"I know," I said, "but my guys didn't realize that, and they had guns."

"I know," said the guide, "but the funny thing is those kitchimookmaan didn't really see that, didn't understand that they just about got shot."

"They told us what they thought happened," said the outfitter, "and when we told them what nearly happened they still didn't believe us. The loudmouth was bragging that he told you to 'fuck off!' and I told him you saved his life. Listen, I've talked to them; they are all city guys, they don't know anything. Of course you can camp anywhere you like. There is an old abandoned camp just down the way, nobody's there, and you know these guys on the island they just hunt from the water or watch crossings; they don't dare go in the bush."

I had a feeling that that was about as long a speech as the outfitter had made in a long time. "It's okay," I said. "We'll go back to Big Trout; it's a real good place.

Anyway, we don't want to hunt where there are a bunch of other guys. Especially them."

"Well, I talked to them," said the outfitter.

We went back down the portage trail, down onto the rock pond, past the old chute, down the rocky portage trail to where the Sauble River was navigable again, and camped on the west arm of Big Trout. We camped there in the night while the bull moose rutted around us—roaring, grunting males on three sides. I watched the deadly tension drift out of my men, and slink back in till they grunted and roared in the night, swilling rum and coughing out quiet challenges like lions toward Long Lake.

Hunting Accident

He sat in the kitchen of the old farmhouse. A single powerful light bulb glared on the ceiling and a hot fire huffed in the furnace. The gale hammered and tapped on the windows, and finding its way only partially barred crept in shivers of cold over his back. Not that he minded.

The real cold in him was anger—fear. He pushed away his plate of congealed bacon, eggs and fried potatoes. Once their aroma had broken into his preoccupation he'd suspected that he would be unable to finish the two full frying pans. He regretted the waste, even at a time like this.

It wasn't his fault, damn it! Maybe Jones was lying. Maybe the grinning bastard had never told Watts, despite what he said. "I told him, and old Watts just sat there, a bottle of beer in his hand, and didn't move. Not for a long time." He said Watts just sat there until his cigarette burned down to his fingers, and for a long second afterward.

But Jones was full of shit, and his sense of humour

was small and black, even if he could tell a good story. Anyways, Jones didn't know himself, not for sure anyway.

Watts was due. They had made this date last week: Opening day, come hell or high water.

The clock hands crawled toward five-thirty. He shrugged and got his stuff together: toilet paper rolled up in a plastic bag, license and tag in another bag, cartridges in their pouch, knife, the rifle and the case. Ah, the rifle. Was the 30-30 the right choice? The shooting would be close, and snow for tracking blood. A scope might fog up. But the Ought Six had more knock-down power. Hell, the 30-30 would do. Better safe than fancy. Oh, the compass. The raging south wind made direction finding a minor problem. He put it on anyway.

Maybe Watts wouldn't show up. As if the thought was a negative charm, he saw the headlights in the driveway.

He pulled on his wool pants, jacket and hat—all red checkered. Not a safe outfit. If he wore fluorescent orange nobody could say they shot him by accident, but somebody would anyway, and guys got away with it all the time. Besides the deer could see that orange; it shone white. Still, with the snow and all? No! Safer with the plaid, and just not be seen. Deer weren't the only problem today.

He walked out to the waiting truck—long and black; its lights reflecting on the blowing snow and the tossing cedars beside his house. The cab was warm, but the windows weren't clear yet. Watts was staring ahead along the lights, both hands gripping the wheel. Bob stepped up into the truck, trying to think of something to say. When he did his voice sounded dry and croaky—"The Ridges?"

"Yah. What are you carrying?" Watts put the truck in reverse, turning to look behind him with his arm on the back of the seat. His eyes as they slid by Bob were inscrutable and swift.

"The 94. You?" He saw that Watts was dressed in a woodland camo coverall with a drab red toque on his head. "You going in dressed like that?"

Watts patted a blaze orange jacket lying like a blanket on the back of the seat. "I'm carrying the 870 with SSG. It's going to be close and lots of gads."

It wasn't far to the Gullies. They were nearly there when they pulled out of the driveway. A mile down the road Bob cleared his throat. "Watts?"

"Yah?" Watts glanced at him. The wipers swatted at the snow driven across the windshield. "Well what?"

Bob breathed in deeply, then exhaled. "You going in the west end?"

"Yah. You want off here, I guess." He snapped off the ends of his words, and pulled over by the side of the road.

"You parking at the gravel pit?" Bob stepped out, uncasing his rifle. The sky was brighter in the east.

"The gravel pit." Watts put the truck in gear. "See you there at lunch, if I don't see you in the Ridges first."

Bob gently pushed the door shut. The truck pulled away. "Maybe I'll see you first. Yah, I better see you first."

Of course Watts couldn't hear him although he could always lie to himself after and say he had. Was Watts joking even blacker than Jones? Had Jones told him at all? Watts was acting funny. Or was he? Maybe he was just sort of seeing Watts from a new, different angle. Maybe Watts meant nothing at all. Maybe.

His tight Kaufmann rubbers made no sound even though he was walking downwind and not consciously trying to be silent. He slipped the shells into the rifle and chambered a round, letting the hammer down to its half notch. He folded between two waving spruce and disappeared from view of the road.

There was an old logging road there and he went quickly up it to the top of the first ridge. The Ridges ran parallel to the road — eight of them. The gullies were choked with spruce and cedars, the tops were bottle-bottom pine, poplar and oaks. Bare rock in long stretches. Completely silent going, but very exposed.

The deer would be tucked on the north side out of the wind, in pockets of cedar. Watts had carried his shotgun. He would be down close to the bush, in the bottom looking for an upwind shot. He would track one if it moved. That was his nature; he never sat still. Bob would find an open area in a gully perhaps, where an escape saddle went through the Ridges. He would watch for the deer that Watts was moving. They didn't try to organize anything anymore. It never worked out anyway. Besides the deer wouldn't leave the gullies on a day like this. They often got one — Watts more than he. Watts was a great still hunter. He usually saw Bob first, and he'd whistle and grin. Not today. Bob wondered what it would feel like. He shuddered. He would have to be very careful.

The first watch he came to was a bare rock knob with a little open marsh north of it. Tag alders crowded the edge of the snow-covered swamp grass. He had established this spot years before. His seat was a piece of broken flat rock on the marsh side of the knob. A spruce beside the seat was denuded of branches halfway up where he had made seats for himself. It was no good today.

Not because the roaring south wind would give away his position; it was too rough for that. Besides, the air currents would be rising in the morning. The only deer that would smell him would be on the far ridge — too far for the 30-30 anyway. No, it was no good because he was exposed here, especially if someone knew that he sat here often.

He clambered down the edge of the rock and with a couple of crunches was through the fringe of tag alders. He stopped at the edge and checked again for deer. Yes, he grinned grimly. Even at a time like this he was still hunting deer.

There was no way that Watts could be here yet, and he was halfway across the little dry marsh before he realized he was leaving a trail obvious from either ridge. Would Watts track him? Probably. "Okay, good!" He cut a little to the right as he climbed through the spruce, birch and poplar. There was a game trail going through a gut in the ridge. He saw an old set of tracks made last night. Just dints in the snow now. He ignored them, but they followed the same trail as he. In the shelter of the cedar gut he saw they were going the other way — into the wind naturally.

The pass narrowed as he climbed until it squeezed between two shoulders of rock where the ridge strained to meet. Here was another track, fresher but still indistinct. A doe by the looks. She had come down the south edge of the ridge and slipped between these rocks as he had. A perfect ambush, but also perfect range for buckshot. He hiked on, on the track of the doe. Not because he wanted her, but because she would show him the runways.

Could Watts be this far yet? No, probably not. Bob wondered if Watts was wearing the fluorescent jacket, because if he remembered correctly, the jacket was reversible — the inside the same red and black plaid as his.

The gut opened into a down hill slope. Big trees, oaks and maples. Thick spruce to the right and left. A maple bush down below with a sugar road running down the centre. This was what they called The Main Gut. He cut back up west on to the top of the ridge where he could watch his back track and the road. In the shelter of some little spruce a log was lying conveniently. He broke some spruce boughs and settled down to watch, his back safely against the overhanging rock. It was a different day here, still drab and drafty, but warm and quiet compared to the tumult on the ridge top.

His position was almost a ground blind. He tried aiming his rifle and found that aiming at the road he could rest on his knee. Just as well. It would be a long shot for iron sights, a hundred and fifty metres down the slope. He wouldn't have to worry about holding low though, the 30-30 would be dropping by then anyway. She would do nicely. She was right on the money at a hundred paces. He was a good shot, and there were no gads to deflect a bullet, just a few big obvious trees — anything on the road was dead. A shot at his backtrail wasn't so good. He would have to twist around to the right. He should be facing that way, he knew. While still having a good shot at the road, he'd have a much better shot at the back trail. But the log was comfortable, and if he were going to sit still, he would have to be comfortable.

He sat still, and kind of disappeared. Oh, he was still in sight, but he meshed and blended in so well that a gang of sharp-eyed schoolboys could have trooped past him on the little sugar road without their minds telling them what their eyes had seen. Certainly a fisher busy on his bloodthirsty weasely business noticed nothing wrong. Nor did a circling raven whose wings whoosh-whooshed over Bob's head. It was nearly full light now. It wouldn't get much brighter. He sat and put his ears and eyes on automatic while his mind wandered back to the woman, the bed, Jones's grinning face, and Watts out there with that damn shotgun.

Twice a suspicious crack came from up on the ridge. Birch bark flittered on a tree, and the wind paced up and down behind him. He was not fooled. He watched and he waited. This is what he was good at. This is what kept his freezer full from fall to fall, and it seemed appropriate that this is how he would live or die. Die or shoot a twenty-year friend. "God damn her for a conniving bitch! Damn the booze and especially damn Jones!" He should shoot them instead of Watts. But Watts was who it would have to be. Watts or him.

He slipped his bare shooting hand inside the front of his coat to keep it nimble and warm. A partridge strutted out of the spruce down to the left, looked around and beetled back in. "Good," he thought, "a sentry." That flank was covered now. All he had to do was wait.

Time dragged by. He was cold. His head nodded. He always got sleepy on a cold watch. His toes were frozen. He flexed them in the rubbers, forcing circulation. He clenched and tightened his muscles, not moving externally but generating heat.

Crash! Off to the right a tree fell and he jumped in his skin — a tenth of a second before his mind told him what it was the rifle was in his hands, cocked, halfway up. He didn't remember doing it.

He realized that the snow had stopped. He wasn't sure when. It had swirled off the top of the ridge for a while, but now there was none in the air. Had the wind died too?

He was wide-awake now, and a lot warmer. He nestled back down into himself and waited. If he turned his head, it was slowly, but all the time his eyes scanned the background. Click, they registered on the road. Click, to the mouth of the gut. Click, to the top of the ridge. "What was that in the gut?"

Something had moved in the cedars at the mouth of the gut. His peripheral vision had picked it up. His eyes searched every chink in the nearly impenetrable wall of cedar. Something had moved. Not a tree in the wind. It was quiet down there. His heart pounded. He forced himself to quiet down, to sit still.

There were branches moving down more to the right now. He turned, forcing cramped muscles to move slowly and fluidly. He wished he had his scoped rifle. He knew it was Watts on his track. Watts moving like a ghost. Not a sound that a man could hear. So quiet that even the deer, if they heard him at all, would think him just another sneaky buck.

Yes, that sneaky — that slow.

Bob's rifle was half way up. Not so far that it would tire him, make him shake — just in position to mount. His thumb was on the hammer and his finger curled around the trigger. He could cock it quietly that way.

Nothing moved. Watts would be standing in the cover, checking the relative open of the hardwoods before he stepped out. Sharp-eyed Watts scanning. Bob shrunk down to his knees, his silhouette now lower. Just his face with its burning eyes over the little spruce in front of him. He caught himself breathing hard and forced his muscles to relax again. He couldn't panic. No buck fever now.

It was eighty or a hundred metres to the cedars. Too far for buckshot, but then again he didn't want to be hit with even one peckle. Did Watts have slugs with him? Those deadly Brenneke slugs would work just fine at this range. Why would Watts be watching an area a hundred metres away if he didn't have slugs? Unless he'd seen that Bob's trail didn't go on across the hardwood and realized that he was being hunted right back.

Behind him the partridge exploded out of the little spruce down by the road. Years of wingshooting reflexes took over. He turned, shouldering the gun — the biggest buck he had ever seen was standing, looking down the road, head and neck visible past the spruce. The rifle found his eye. The sights settled on the base of the deer's swollen neck, and before he realized what he had done, the rifle roared. The buck crumpled — his huge rack bouncing once off the forest floor before settling back on his shoulder.

Watts was standing clear of the cedars — the

shotgun in his hand. Bob whirled back around, knowing he was too late, off balance and dead meat. Knowing even as he was about to die, that his last act had been to shoot a trophy buck.

"Nice shot!" shouted Watts. "I have been watching that big son-of-a-bitch for the last five minutes. He was down the road too far for the shotgun. I knew damn well you were around here somewhere. Great deer! Do you want to gut him out or should we go get the truck? I have a camera in the truck. Maybe we should get it first. I can drive right up the sugar road. Let's go look at him. Boy, have you ever got buck fever! You should see your face!"

The Coat

He'll come to my coat." John threw his plaid jacket on the snow.

I rolled a cigarette. "Well he's no damn good." I peered at John under the brim of my hat. "You might as well shoot him."

John shrugged. "A gun shy dog's no good." He spread the coat out. "Specially a hound."

"I know." I opened the action of my pump shotgun a bit just to make sure there was a shell in it. "Want me to shoot him?"

"No!" John slid his shotgun into the crook of his arm. "It won't work anyway, not with us here. Not with the guns."

I nodded toward the lengthening shadow of the big spruce as it crawled across the snow toward the jacket. "Be dark soon anyway. Could be a while before he comes."

"Be morning probably," said John. "He'll be here in the morning. He'll be tired of chasing useless rabbits by then, cold and hungry. He'll come to the coat."

I spat. "Screwed up a good day of hunting, he did."

Now I never did much like hunting with hounds anyway. I didn't like the fast buckshot shooting, the imperfection of it. I didn't like the panic in the deer's eyes and the adrenaline that lingered in the meat. I did it only because John loved his hounds and he was my friend, and I did it because of the music of it. It drifted in now — far away, a deep baritone. "That's him?"

John nodded, "Oh yes." He sighed. "Prettiest voiced hound I ever owned — rabbit chasing, cowardly fool!"

I shrugged. "I don't much like hounds anyway, kept on a chain, stupid, smelly, jump up. You know..." I sort of trailed off.

John buttoned his cotton shirt tight up to his chin. "Hounds ain't like your collie, for sure. You can't talk to a hound, not and be understood. But no cattle dog ever sounded like that. Listen."

And I listened. The distant solitary voice drifted in among the darkening conifers and entered the skin of my arms. It played over my shoulders and ruffled the hair on the back of my neck. "Maybe we could keep him for rabbits?"

John scoffed, "I'm not keeping a Redbone hound for rabbits. Besides he's gun shy."

"I'll take him."

He smiled. "You don't even like hounds. Besides what would you do with him? Keep him on a chain? He can't run loose." He flapped his arms at his side to generate heat. "What kind of life would that be for him, never being able to hunt? Remember when you went down to work in Toronto? You came back for hunting season, even though it meant your job. Remember that?"

I remembered that. "Isn't he getting closer?"

"No, he is hot on some bunny's tail up on that poplar ridge. He's gaining on him. Sees him I figure." John turned. "We might as well go; he'll be on the coat in the morning."

"You going to catch him first, John?"

John was already trudging away, the snow squeaking under his boots. "Well, he won't be hard to catch. He'll be glad to see me, as long as I don't have a gun. But that is not what I am going to do. I'll sneak in. The wind will be seeping up the ridge. He won't smell me, and I'll shoot him from up there with my rifle."

"You couldn't catch him first. Be more" — I searched for the right word — "exact."

John shook his head. "Poor bugger's so gun shy he would be scared at the end like. It's better if I do it from up there."

"What about your coat, won't it get all bloody?"

John looked back at the new plaid jacket glowing red on the bluing snow. "I don't want it any more."

I too looked at the jacket, warm, secure, smelling of John no doubt, and dogs, woodsmoke and home. "I guess he can keep it, eh John?"

John nodded soberly and walked silently up the ridge. He had his shotgun clamped under one arm and his hands jammed in his pockets. He sure looked cold without his coat.

Chains

The wolves slipped down in the dark, down into the cold, open fields. They were a family— grandmother, mother, father, and three mostly grown pups. Even in the dark, they didn't lope across the open, but hung to whatever cover there was—the regrown spruce where rabbits sometimes hid, down into the shelter of a gully, hip deep and quiet, up through some cattails close to one of the houses beside the road.

The three adults lay here with their bellies tight on the crust, waiting in a grassy fence line for the pups to catch up. The pups could be heard yip yipping as foolishly as dogs, and as unlikely as dogs to catch a snowshoe rabbit, not on the winter snow like this— *"All squeal, no meat."* The wolves turned into fence posts or clumps of grass, as frozen still as their surroundings. The stupid dog that lived here couldn't see them, couldn't smell them for they were downwind, but he barked anyway, an inarticulate moron arfing that affected them not at all. He was on a chain—*"Chains catch, chains hold."*

If the stupid big dog had been off the chain, he would no doubt have followed them, back into the bush away from the fields of men, where, who knows, they might have taken him down. But he was a big dog, and they were small wolves; not coyotes, but not timber wolves either. Still, they sang like wolves and they smelled like wolves and they kept the rule of the dominant pair like wolves — so they were wolves. But he was a big dog, even if he was a moron; besides he was on a chain, staked beside the house. The man that lived here never responded to his barking and the pack often came close in the dark, hunting cats. They smelled no cats tonight. The male might have held the dog for them to finish, for he was big with hair more than fur, and was certainly part dog himself. Still he was born of a wolf, and raised by a wolf, and his pups were wolves, so he too was a wolf.

The three pups came skidding in, spraying the adults with snow. The little female prostrated herself in front of her grandmother, rolling her belly toward her, she who had never been shown a tooth; and her brother sat, exposing his wider chest and hair-like fur, so like his father — *"A touch of dog there."* Their bigger sister came and sat beside the adults, as still as they. She, unlike the other pups, had her grandmother's great voice, the warble of a true timber wolf, although still juvenile in timbre.

With the three pups firmly in control, the wolves single-filed toward the next farmstead in the big open space. The grandmother went first, keeping to the gully where the sun hit in the day and the snow was fast, but down out of sight of any watcher. She didn't bother checking for anything at the apple tree and looked disapprovingly when the male thought of it. They came to a soft deep drift where the gully narrowed. The male plunged ahead and she followed. Behind were the three pups, with their mother shepherding them along — *"This is no time for foolishness."*

This was a more dangerous place, with more potential for reward. The grandmother stopped at a woven wire fence. It was clean of man smell, but *"Wire snares, wire chokes."* They floated over the low spot, swung through a cross gully and worked their way downwind. The dog here was wolf-like himself, big and smart; they knew him well and respected his diligence and ferocity. He would never chase them far from help, and his help was horrible and definite.

The man here had killed those of the pack before. The first had been the grandmother's sister, long ago, loping in the evening at what should have been a safe distance. He had shot and broken her like a back-bitten rabbit. And the old bitch's mate, he had killed him too, in the night — the man was often out with his flashlight. They had been feeding on a dead calf when the light had come on and the shot had roared. Her mate had run away beside her, but he had several small hot holes in him and he had died before dawn. This was a very dangerous place, but there were often dead calves smelling of medicine, or old cows just dead, or piles of guts smelling of the man — and the wolves were hungry.

The dog was getting older. He was older than the grandmother could remember, stiff, but he would fight hard — *"A meal is wasted if you're hurt."* It would be better to try the little bitch at the farm across the corner.

She was young and smaller, and might be tempted out. If they had been timber wolves instead of brush wolves with pretensions they might have tried her. Instead they fanned out across the crest of the hill and watched for the dog and the puddle of light that moved with the man if he went out to the cattle. *"Don't bother cattle, they all charge."*

It was doubly important to stay upwind for there were other dogs here, strange exotic things that could smell them at great distances and then bay with unbelievable voice. These two dogs were seldom off their chains. *"Chains hold."*

When they were loose they chased coons, though even the grandmother could not understand why. *"A coon if you're hungry"* — but coons fight hard and taste bad. Still, the two floppy-eared dogs would chase the coon, bellowing in their booming voices until the coon treed and then the man would shoot it out of the tree with a pop gun. It seemed to please the dogs, though not as much as catching the coon on the ground. The grandmother wanted nothing to do with those two dogs and was glad they were on the chains.

The hounds did not smell them tonight, the farm dog did not patrol and chase them off, and the man who lived here did not come out and check the cattle as yet. The grandmother lolled her tongue and studied the buildings. The cattle were lying down; she could smell no dead, nor taste on the air any afterbirth. None smelled close to calving. Still it was worth watching; there might be something just out of wind. Perhaps a cat would come by, out in the open away from the dog. The dog might be in the house.

Or he could be lying with the cattle.

It would be better to let the man come out, and the dog if it was with him. It was usually with him. Then when they went back in, it would be safer for a little while. The man might be hiding in the round bales, with the light and the gun. *"Never look at the light, the light shows."*

The windows of the house were dark. That was a good thing, except that it meant that the dog was probably outside, and when he barked the man was close behind. This was a man to be feared; he could squeal like a wounded rabbit. Hearing it once, she was only saved because a fox had died first, and she had read the sign, and smelled the blood and the man.

He would work with the dogs, and the dogs with him. The dogs drove foxes to him and coons up trees and the farm dog was always with him. They chased the cattle sometimes as a team. She had seen it many times, lying on the edge of the brush out of sight but in touch.

Once the dog had cut them off, forcing them to either run past the man in the house yard, or out onto the ploughed gravel road. She had felt trapped, them all running in the open, but he hadn't seen them— *"Men see poor in the dark."* He had known they were there. The dog told him and he had the gun but he couldn't shoot them. He had roared, not the silly babble noise that men make, but a voice that bellowed out and spoke of territory and ownership.

They lay there, stretched out in a row, outside the yardlight's white puddle, up where cattle sometimes winter and old bull thistles and burdocks break the flat expanse of the snow. Even the pups were still. The man came out without the dog. He walked to the cattle with his portable light. Its yellow beam probed them once, but they were too far, and looked away — *"Never look at the light."* The man spoke to the cattle, but the dog did not come. He pushed a calf under the burning wire, and a cow bawled and shook her head at him, but the dog did not threaten her. Finally the man turned his light and walked slowly back to the house. The dog did not run to get in with him.

The lights went off in the windows of the house. The wolves rose and trotted just downwind of the cattle.

Then they smelled the dog-blood. The dog was dead. The dog had been shot in the head. The smell of the man was on his death — *"The man has killed the dog."* They ate him. He was tough and skinny, but they ate him and even licked the bloody snow. *"The man killed the dog."*

No more would the dog follow the man around the farm. He would not chase the cattle when they were outside the fence, and lie beside the calves when they were not. He would never tell of the wolves' presence again, nor chase them off. Instead he had filled their drawn-up bellies.

The wolves took a different path out of the clearance. *"Only foolish deer make trails."* They crested the height of the bare rocks above the farms and sat together in the frosty darkness. Below, the farmyard lights made puddles of brightness around the dark buildings. Moved by strange emotions, the old female lifted her muzzle and howled. Her daughter joined in with her poor reedy voice, and the male with his dog-influenced harshness. The pups yodeled in unison. Over to the north a pack of huskies chained in their

yards—speedy slave-pullers of men—answered
twenty strong with nearly wolf-like voices. They spoke
of the race and ride and the feeding ritual. The moron
tied in his yard ark arked along. He had nothing to
say but territory, and the little female at the next farm
spoke of her duty and her diligence. Her voice was
surpassingly good—northern dog strain. The hounds
in the farmer's yard voiced long mournful syllables,
round sounds like the chain links that held them. They
spoke of the hunt and the fight, and the sweet smell of
a hot track. They spoke of how the chain held them or
they would hunt. The wolves spoke back of their hunt,
and their territory, and how they were together. A pack
of despicable coyotes by the river warbled, claiming
territory for themselves, and bragging of their
numbers, and just as it all faded in volume, far far away
over in the mountains a lone timberwolf raised his
voice in glory. The wolves sang of how they were
healthy and how they held this territory. They spoke
of the chase, and the night, and the sanctity of blood.

The singing nearly died away; only the distant
coyotes and a few huskies were still calling when they
saw the moving puddle of light come out into the
farmer's yard. It swept around the cattle. The distant
timberwolf howled again and the hounds bawled out
an answer. The voices carried to the mountains of the
wolf, and with the wolf's reply came rolling back.
Intertwining like the northern lights, the huskies to
the north couldn't be out of it, nor could the wolves. It
rang like a lament over the canine range. A distant
house dog howled in the dead air, a faint calliope
heralding the spread of the sing-sing. Then a new voice
joined the chorus; a bit like a timberwolf it was, with a

hint of northern dog. *"That is the man."* The grandmother tilted her head. She raised her muzzle and sang of loss and life, the cold and the kill. She let her voice twine with his, while the chorus sang around them, and the night beat with it until it dropped off with a few last yips of the huskies. The old female turned away, toward the spruce-warm swamp. *"Chains — he spoke of chains."*

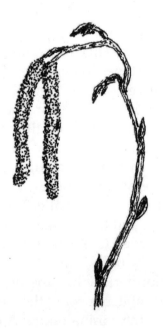

The Wolfer

That Wolfer came around today again. Maw had always said not to pay any attention to him, just look right through him, like he didn't exist. That's what she does. I never once seen her let her eyes rest on him at all, even if he wasn't looking — of course he was always looking. That's what she would say, under her breath, "There he is, lookin!"

Of course we were not supposed to look at him, none of us, not Maw, not me, Jimmy or Alice, we were all supposed to just focus on something way behind his back. Maw said it just like that, "You look real hard at something right on the other side of him. You look so hard that you can see it right through him. That's the way you look at him, as if he wasn't there, as if there was sort of something that caught your attention, but it was way past him, way more important than him."

You know, even if he was there I think there were lots of times that we just didn't see him, not at first, but if he was upwind you could sure smell him. He snared the wolves, or shot them, but mostly he poisoned them, strychnine on a dead animal; of course I guess that didn't work so well, now that the buffalo were all rotted away. All that skinning musky wolves, and handling dead meat, and the fact that he didn't wash very careful and maybe he wanted to stink anyway, like a wolf — all that made the horses rear it did, and our milk cow throw up her head, and our dog snarl and Maw stop whatever it was she was doing and look through him till he went away.

I was never as good at it as her, the looking through him I mean. Not as good as my older brother and sister — they had it down. They could stand there one on each side of her and stare him down. When I was real little Maw'd hold on to my shoulders and face me toward him, and I'd do it too, until his eyes would sort of slide down to me. He wouldn't do anything, no silly face like some adults, no wink, no smile, he wouldn't change expression, as if he too were participating in the silly looking game. As if damn it that's why he'd walked the mile or so from his place, just to have a look. But even though I was supposed to be looking through him, he'd catch me, and I'd be looking at him, then he'd sort of look at me. So it got so that I didn't stand in front of Maw when they were staring at him, and I don't know if it was my idea that I should always just go off a ways, or maybe it was Maw's; it might even have been his.

It developed into a pattern. I'd see him first, out in front of our house just off the lot line, under that little brushy hill, standing behind the ditch gads fifty metres or so from the house, not trying to hide but just naturally hard to see. I'd always see him though, then

I'd walk to Maw or Jimmy or Alice and sort of twitch
my head that way, and then they'd know to line up
across the front of the house, or if they were inside
Maw'd be at the door and one of them at each window.
If I had been inside when he came, I wouldn't have
seen him, but I was never inside when he came, or if I
was they didn't notice him.

He was old, older than Maw for sure, not as old as
Granpa or Mr. MacDougal our other neighbour but
old, probably thirty-five or maybe even forty. When I
was a little kid, I was scared of him. Maw would say,
"There's the Wolfer!" and I'd hide, so would Jimmy
and Alice. When I think about it, it was me that first
came out and looked at him, not one of them. Maw
had said, "Get back now!" but I hadn't. That's when
she told me about how I was supposed to look at him
as if he was just a transparent obstacle to my vision.

The one time I ever got Jimmy to say anything
about it we were hauling in a quarter of moose that
the Wolfer had hung by our drive. We were sliding it
in on the snow, and Jimmy was still mad at Maw. We
went and got the hindquarter, but she had said not
to—"Leave it rot!" she'd said. "Just because the son-
of-a-bitch has shot more meat than he can eat, doesn't
mean we have to nose around his leavins." She had
said it loud so that if there was any chance that the
Wolfer was within earshot he'd have heard. "Leave it
for the ravens!"

"Bull shit!" said Jimmy. "I like moose and we've
been out of meat for a week!" He nodded toward me
and we went out with the toboggan to haul it in.

"I'll whip you!" screamed Maw.

"Then you do it!" he said, "but when you're done

Alice will cook it up for us. Won't you Alice?"

Alice said she would, and Maw had just shrugged.

We let it down out of the tree; I coiled the rope and hung it on the limb, but Jimmy took it down and tied the quarter on the toboggan so the snow wouldn't slide it off. "I'll bring it back later," he said.

"Why does Maw hate him?" I asked.

"He beat up Dad."

"Is that why he left, our Dad?" I looked over at Jimmy; he was straining against the rope, older than me and a lot bigger than me, wide shouldered and heavy for a boy.

"I don't know." Jimmy looked down to check the footing, and kept looking there. "It might have been, he left right after that. Alice said they were yelling, I don't remember that, but she said that finally the Wolfer pushed back his chair and said that they would have to talk about that outside and that there was nothing more to say about it indoors in front of the kids."

Jimmy slid to his knees and panted, "Are you pulling your weight? This damn quarter can't be that heavy." He knelt there looking at the ground like a spent dog. "I asked Alice what they were yelling about but she said she only really started listening to the words when the Wolfer said that they shouldn't speak them in front of kids. By then it was just the men yelling and Maw crying. I remember that, and Maw screaming. I guess you don't remember none of that do you?"

I reached over and helped him up. "I don't remember Dad at all." I noticed that Jimmy's face was wet. "He left right after that?"

"The next day." Jimmy pulled at the rope on the toboggan, his hand slid up the rope to mine. "Come on, together now! One, two, three, pull!"

That's the way they always said it, Maw, Jimmy or Alice, always the same thing, trying to fix a fence post, or setting up a gate, or dragging a bag of potatoes from the garden—"One, two, three." That and the lining up to stare through the Wolfer. I guess I was about ten or twelve when I got to thinking about how stupid that was. By that time Jimmy was pretty much a man, and the Wolfer didn't come around as often. Alice got married and moved away and pretty much the only time I saw the Wolfer was when I went hunting. I'd be sneaking along and I'd look over and there he'd be looking at me; he'd just nod at first, and without them around I'd just nod back.

One day he said, "Why don't you go around that way, and I'll go up on the ridge; if we jump anything one of us will see it for sure!"

I had seen this man my whole life, and I knew that he was able to talk, but that was the first time I heard it, and he spoke as if we'd been just carrying on a conversation a minute ago. And I guess we had been communicating, because he had walked parallel with me on the other side of the draw and once even waved his hand that I should go over farther.

He didn't like my old single-shot shot gun; I knew he didn't, just the way he looked at it. He had a 25-35 Winchester just right for wolves and not bad on bigger stuff if you were a real good shot, which he was. I never heard him shoot more than twice and he shot some pretty big stuff, bears, wolves, deer and moose. He said he even shot the last buffalo he ever saw with it.

"Get a rifle!" is all he said to me.

Jimmy knew I was hunting with the Wolfer, but he never said anything against it, and he never told Maw, and I think that maybe if the Wolfer had come and stood at the gate that Jimmy wouldn't have played the looking game, not anymore.

But the next time the Wolfer came and stood at our driveway was when I was fourteen, and then he stood there with an extra pack and a .22 Hornet rifle, and looked at me—and I had shaken Jimmy's hand, hugged Maw and said, "Goodbye Maw, I'm going with the Wolfer."

Trading

They look alike, the people of the island, not that there is anything unusual in that. People on islands or in small, isolated communities are often interrelated. But the people here are very related. A wry observer, if one could be found, say, paddling up the marsh in a big freighter canoe, might think them all brothers. And if they lifted their pale faces and blinked softly with their faint blue eyes he might hiss softly to himself, "or sisters," as his canoe caresses, then rips into the soft mud of the sloping shore.

They don't help, these islanders; they seem inclined to run, or cry, or at least break into a serious pout, but not to grab a bow, or pull a line, or — heaven forbid — shoulder a pack. "No," thought the swarthy dwarf (for so one such wry observer appeared beside the tall slender blondes gazing petulantly all around him), "no" — he mulled it over in his mind — "they will not attack either, not at first, not in my face at least."

No one spoke, not the trader, nor even the old man with billowing white hair, who shuffled toward him on bony legs. He wore light leather shorts, braces and sandals; the rest of him was pasty gray skin, approaching in a wobbling dance across the sandy beach.

"Christ!" said the trader, but all the dim eyes he tried to meet were turned to the old man who stopped, still, exactly one body length away.

The old man's eyes crawled up the trader. Starting at his knee high moccasins, they moved up his thighs, brown with homespun, darted around the groin, made a brave attempt to land on the deerskin jacket but whizzed on by it, then quick as a dragonfly, snip, they met the trader's eyes and were gone—had retreated, and now nestled by their owner's scabby feet.

The trader whistled through his flowing black mustache, cleared his throat, and whispered, "I have trade goods: needles, files, fish hooks, axes, knives, powder, shot"—a couple of sets of dull blue eyes flashed momentarily toward him—"pots, pans, guns... I have two guns..." The sun mirrored in more thin faces, a series of flickering blinks among the blond, wafting, long-haired band of them.

More were coming all the time. One of the newcomers must have been important because the rest parted sullenly and let him through. He was not fat, or muscular, nor was he one of the elders. The trader couldn't see anything special about him, or even recognizable for that matter. Still, the tall spindly youths, the waif-like girls and the more shrunken adults made way for him without even looking up, as if he had an aura—which he didn't; not in the trader's view at least.

"Hi!" wasn't answered, not at first, not before

glaring in the direction of one little dark-haired girl who was hunched defensively behind the billowing dress of her mother. Then as if it were an awful responsibility, as if — damn it — every one expected this of him, the man answered.

"Hi..." He looked at the old man, he glanced at the trader, and he seemed to run out of conversation.

The trader decided not to look directly at them; he was scaring them, or embarrassing them or something, whatever. It was not good for business and survival. "You got anything to trade?"

Was that too abrupt? Might that be a suggestion of poverty? For all the trader knew a blue eye might be nestled right now on a set of sights and could be caressing his side. He glanced toward a grove of tended sugar maples. Sure enough, a tall scrawny figure in a breech cloth was leaning over a low limb, the rifle just a black hole with a brown rim at the bottom. "Well," he murmured, "at least something here will look you in the eye."

"Mmmm?" said the important guy, and his eyes slid down the line of the trader's sight to the tree. As if his face were a big signal the man at the maples put down the rifle and walked toward them, into the midst of them, and began mumbling occasionally and glancing back and forth now and then, like the rest.

"Well, you talk it over, and I'll move over here, downwind like, and have a pipe, so's not to bother you." He didn't think he should go down to the canoe to get his punk burning in its can. That could scare them, they could think he was going for a gun, or running away, or... God knows. Besides he would have to walk back up again. They might have to organize all over again for that.

"Say," he reached in his pouch and pulled out a shiny needle stuck through a piece of leather as thick as his grimy thumbnail, "I'll trade a needle for a hot coal, and something to eat and drink." He held out his grossly big tobacco pouch. "Anybody want to try my mix?"

A couple of the older men flicked their eyes toward their wives, who maybe lowered a downy eyebrow a bit, but no one wanted a smoke he guessed.

The little dark-haired girl turned and went back through them and they shrunk from her touch as she brushed past them. She trotted away from them up the slope to the low log houses tucked in among the spruce near the top. Sheep startled as she ran.

The trader looked at the strange light-fleeced sheep, then at the people's clothing. "Say, that's not cotton you're wearing, it's wool." He tried to conceal his excitement. "Nice weaving! I wondered where you had traded for cotton. I'll trade for some of that light wool." He caught himself just as he was about to lick his lips. "Yah, I can trade with that."

They traded — lengths of woven wool, fine and soft as the women's hair, new white garments, rolls of yarn finer than he thought possible, heavier stuff for outdoor wear, shirts, pants and dresses, all nicely done with subtle patterns woven in with darker shades of wool. And no colour in any of it.

The little girl came with a bucket; her eyes met his, but she looked away when disapproving glances bore in from each side. He took the bucket and she scurried away. "Wait," he said, "your needle!"

She dashed back and took it, flashing him a little

grin. He heard murmuring behind him. The big shot cleared his throat a couple of times, shuffled his feet and shrugged. A cold chill went down the trader's back. "I'll come back again, if you want me to. I don't guess you get a lot of traders. When was the last time — six, seven years ago?" A bunch of eyes snapped at him; as many flared at the little girl.

The trader lifted both his hands and ducked his head, consciously keeping his eyes down around his own moccasins. He checked in the wooden bucket that the girl had brought: cold mutton, an old wine bottle full of...water, and a smudge. He lit his pipe, took a bite of fine ground bread and overcooked sheep and chewed, swallowed and smoked all at the same time. The islanders expressed interest — sort of; younger men glanced at older men, and the long backs of the older women got a bit stiffer. The trader brushed his pants of crumbs and took a slug of water. His Adam's apple, covered in black quarter-inch stubble, bobbed; he wiped his mustache with the back of his sleeve — to hell with them. "Sorry I couldn't trade them rifles. I could see some of you fellas were interested..." He pointed to the pile of cloth on the trading hide before him. "I can only take so much wool. I mean I have to carry it, you know."

If they knew they weren't showing it; several of the younger ones looked toward his canoe though and even some of the women exchanged glances.

"Well, if you have anything else, tell me — or show me I guess. If not, I'll go. I expect you'd rather I camped a long way off, for the night...you know."

The old man and the big shot exchanged looks, and he realized that they had let him see that they did, or perhaps they had waited until he was looking their way to briefly make eye contact with each other. Now they both glanced at him.

"Well," he hesitated, "no need to get all excited. I'll be back next year this time. The smith that makes them turns out seven or eight for every trip. I'll always have some more. It's not like you are right out of guns." Several bottom lips got bigger; he swore he saw tears in a few male eyes. "You could tell me what you want—shotgun, rifle—calibre even. I could take custom orders."

Some of the men rung long bony fingers, some lifted their heads a little and glanced at him under their pale brows. The one who had been sighting at him from the maples glared toward the big shot.

"Look, I can't give credit. Not if I am going to stay in this business. Not if I'm going to come back." He emphasized the last part.

They seemed resigned to that, several hairless chests rose in unison. The big shot stepped forward, nearing to a body length, then stopped.

"What?" the trader whispered desperately. He had cleaned them out of wool; they had absolutely nothing else he wanted. Maple sugar was a dirge on the market, wheat was too heavy—they had nothing for him.

The dark eyes of the little girl were on him as she pressed through back to the side of her young mother, who flinched when the child touched her hand.

The big shot looked toward the child. When she met his glance he looked quickly away, back to the trader, down to the ground.

"The last trader to come here, was his name Pouch? Did he have a big tobacco pouch, like mine?"

The big shot nodded almost imperceptibly and the young mother shrank a little more. The little dark-haired girl smiled. The trader didn't smile. He nearly did, but he caught it just under the edges of his moustache.

"Pouch is doing all right; he healed pretty well, stays home now. He has several canoes and a schooner out. Thing is he needs a servant. You don't have anybody interested do you?"

Most of the islanders shuffled uncomfortably.

"Be like an indentured servant, see, learn a trade too, something good for, say, a mother and a child. Two rifles for a year. That's a good deal. They could come back with me next year."

The islanders seemed uncomfortable with the idea. He shrugged. "It was only a notion... If you're worried about me, hell—I'm a married man with a reputation to uphold. I'm not used to dealing in people—I mean nobody does... This one time though, I thought..." His words just hung on the air for a while and then blew away through the crowd of islanders. They seemed to sway as the words passed.

The big shot looked at the mother, he glanced at the canoe, his eyes flicked to the trader.

"She doesn't want to go," said the little girl. "Can I go?" Her little brown eyes held his.

"Well..." the trader stroked his chin, "old Pouch does need someone to do errands for him around the house. I could only give one rifle though, for a year. I suppose I could give both rifles, but it would have to be for a lot longer, till maturity say."

The mother looked at the child. Her hand moved, and then fell down short of touching the thick black hair. She glanced once toward the big shot, and he nodded to the trader.

The child ran back up the hill, brown heels flying from under her dress. The trader had the canoe ready when she came back down with a bundle. Her eyes swept the ring of islanders once and settled momentarily on the stiff form of her mother, then she pushed the dragging bow of the canoe out and hopped into it, sprinkling a trail of water over the canvas load-cover and the grinning trader. "How far is it?"

The Old MacDougal Place

The tractor was an old International 414, dented here and there—but it still ran well. Sure it leaked a little oil, had standard steering, and no brakes to speak of, but the way the farmer saw it, it was still a nice tractor to plough with, specially in little odd-shaped fields like this. It was quick on the headlands and sure-footed. It could plough through wet hollows where his big tractor would have been stuck. Twice already today he had had it standing up on its back wheels pulling the bogged plough loose—like a rearing stallion.

"Come on Baby!" he coaxed, stepping on the differential lock. "Pull her through." He eased up on the depth control a bit and the tractor groaned as it turned up sod against the wet landside.

He glanced at the sprucey horizon. The front was moving in from the west like a solid wall in the sky. The wind was fresher now, promising rain. "The end of October and I'm still not done ploughing." He bit his lip. It was tricky here on the side-hills of the Old

MacDougal place. Snags stuck up everywhere, ridges of raw soil where he had recleared with his loader tractor. He had pushed the brush to the edges of the field to something like the dimensions Old MacDougal had cleared all those years before.

He remembered hunting here when he was a boy; it was grown up with brush even back then. It must have been a nice farm once but when Old MacDougal had died, years before he was born, it had been deserted and no one had farmed here since. It had struck him as a spooky place when he was a boy — in the evening with the light fading on the tumble-down buildings, and the wind waving the tops of the brush in the regrown fields. It had spooked him then, and even now thinking of it he felt a sort of chill, a being-watched feeling. He shrugged it off. He wouldn't scurry home now. He was a man after all, a man behind in his work.

He spotted fresh deer tracks in a bare piece of ground where the loader had scraped off the years' accumulated grass and duff. Deer season started on Monday... "What day is this?" he wondered aloud, his voice just a murmur over the labouring tractor. "Wednesday, Thursday?" It was October 31st, he knew, for his children were getting ready for Halloween. He shook his head. "Hell, 31st and still ten acres to plough."

He saw that he had a bunch of sod and poplar roots caught in the mullboards again, but he couldn't stop here — too steep and the feeble parking brake wouldn't hold. He'd have to muddle through until he crested the knoll. He lifted the plough with its load of jammed trash and headed up on the unploughed sod. The tractor lurched as it momentarily lost its footing on the steep side-hill slope of the gully. He felt that same old grab in the pit of his stomach that it always gave him. "Come on, Girl!" But instead of righting itself as usual, the tractor rolled in what felt like slow motion, and the farmer was under it.

"Don't panic!" he told himself. "Stay calm." He spoke as if he was talking to someone else — a scared boy trapped under a running tractor perhaps. "You don't seem to be hurt, not too bad anyway. Best turn it off." He could reach the kill switch. He pulled it. The wheel above quit turning and the silence settled in.

"Now who is liable to hear that I'm not moving?" He ran through some possibilities in his mind. Not the people on the next place — their new home was so soundproof that they probably didn't know he was here in the first place. His wife was on afternoon shift at the hospital, and the kids would just automatically go to the babysitter's after school. No one could see this little field from the road. "No one will know; no one." He wiggled experimentally; "I'll have to get myself free." But he couldn't. He thought his left leg was broken. It certainly was trapped. "Lots of weight on it." He spoke matter-of-factly, checking to see if there was any fuel spilled. There wasn't, so he rolled a smoke and lit it, inhaling deeply. "Think," he said. "Bleeding a bit." He reached down the leg as far as he could and felt a pant-leg soaked with wet, sticky blood. "Bleeding lots."

He hitched himself up on his elbows and looked around — "I think I'm about to become a statistic." He flicked the butt of the cigarette far out onto the ploughed ground. He watched it arch, and saw a man walking toward him from the west. Relief flooded over him, and then a twinge of disappointment. The road was to the east and if this fellow was coming from the other way he was probably picking mushrooms or something and his car would be far away.

The old man moved well though, because he was kneeling beside him now. "Well, young fellow, you're in a pickle, aren't you?" He was dressed in overalls and work boots. That didn't mean he was a farmer though, or any other kind of labour-skilled man. It was all the fashion now for rich retired yuppies to imitate workingmen's dress.

"Can you dig under me and get my leg free?"

"No, sorry." The old man peered closer, tilting his head to see under the upside down seat. "You are sure trapped under that machine!"

He felt himself losing patience with the old fellow. That wouldn't do. "Reach into the tool kit beside the seat. There is a big crescent wrench there. Hand it to me and I'll dig myself out."

The old man took a deep breath, and fiddled with the lid of the toolbox, but he couldn't seem to open it. "It must be jammed, never mind it." The farmer fought to control his temper. "Maybe you can reach down and try to get the bleeding stopped."

"No, don't see that I can. Sorry." The old fellow seemed to mean well, but this was a hell of a time to get squeamish. There was genuine pity in his voice and in his eyes. He seemed helpless, or addled.

"I guess you better go for help then; it's not far over to the neighbours." He pointed.

The old man shook his head. He had tears in his

eyes. "I can't." He brushed his face with his gnarled old hand. "I am really sorry about it young fella. But I can't do any of that stuff."

"Look! If you don't do something I'm going to bleed to death, right here in front of you. And all your blubbering won't save me."

The old man shook his gray head. "I know and I feel right bad about it too. I mean, you have been doing such a good job clearing this here trash and all..."

"For God's sake, wake up!" he shouted in the old gray face. "You have to do something."

The old man lifted his head as if he heard something. "There's a pair of dogs down in the bottom running deer. Bad dogs, they are, dropped off some time ago, bad dogs. If they smell the blood..."

The farmer felt himself panic. If the crazy old guy was right, both of them were in real danger. That pair of dogs had chased his neighbour up a tree last spring. The whole community was hunting them. "Look, take off, go for help!" he shouted at the old man. "You're not safe either."

"Oh, I'm all right; don't you worry about me. I'll just sit here a bit with you, have a smoke maybe." He pulled out a big corncob pipe and lit it with a wooden match that he struck with his thick thumbnail.

"Roll a smoke for me, will yah?" He handed his makings up.

The old man looked genuinely sad. "I'm sorry, I..."

"Yah, yah, you can't." He rolled one for himself, spilling half the tobacco on his chest. He saw the old man look fascinated at the Bic lighter. "Beats the hell out of me how you got to be your age and never learned to roll, seeing as you smoke and all."

"Now young fella, there's no need to talk like that."
He stood up. "Oh, oh," he said.

The farmer turned his head and saw two big
German shepherd dogs coming upwind toward them,
their heads up tasting the air for his blood. "Shit!" he
shouted. "Take off, just move away, move slow, don't
look back. Go to the neighbours."

"I can't do that," said the old man, and he held up
his hand as the farmer started to speak. "Besides if I
go they will kill you."

"They'll kill you too. Go, they are dangerous."

The old man looked down at him. "I know. Them
I can handle." He stepped over the farmer and walked
toward the dogs, waving his hands. "Away with you!
You damn curs."

The farmer saw the dogs stop, hackles up. He saw
their lips pull back over their gums, showing their long
yellow teeth. "Leave him be, you bastards!" shouted
the farmer. "Here! Get back here, you old fool—they'll
kill you!"

The old man looked back at him and smiled. "No
they won't. Watch this!" He ran toward the dogs,
shouting. They turned and ran for their lives. One
actually yelped. The old man chuckled and returned
to the farmer. "You best hunt them down—when your
leg is better. Half wild like that, they're dangerous."

"You chased them away. Just like that. Outbluffed
them, I guess. Damnedest thing I ever saw!"

"Well, dogs see me you know."

"Of course they see you, you silly brave old fool.
Thank God you were here!"

The old man hunkered down beside him. "I knew
they were around. I had no intention of letting them

get you. Not after you fixing up this place and all. Besides..."

A shot rang out, then another, and another. "You best holler," said the old man. "That's that nice young fella from down the road a bit. He just shot them dogs. He'll hear you if you yell. He's a good boy."

"Randy? How the hell do you know Randy? Where are you from?"

"I have to go now; I scare that Randy if I'm around. If I'm around he leaves, same as you used to. Too bad. I like having you boys around." The old man had a playful look on his face. "You holler now!"

The farmer hollered and he heard Randy answer. When he looked around the old man had slipped away.

"Bill?" shouted Randy from the edge of the bush. "Hell Bill, I'll be right over."

Randy bound his wound and dug him out. "I'll go for help. Do you think any more of those dogs are around? You better keep my rifle. I would sure hate to be helpless here. This place gives me the creeps. Are you sure you'll be all right till I get back?

"Yes," Bill said. "I'll be fine."

Graveyard on Seven-fifty

Ok, I'll admit it. I knew him well. But I haven't seen him for years. We were both raised on this sideroad, and got hired on in the mine about the same time. There were a lot of us in those days who realized we were never going to make a living on the farm like our fathers, so off to the mines.

We worked on the same level. That was before they brought the smoke-puking scoop trams underground, and every level was full of men. He was following a drift crew, roof bolting. They had a special name for what I did — it had to do with our canine companions and sex.

The upper levels of Crean Hill were old; small drifts ran off in strange directions, and it was uncommonly cold, water leaked from the back. Even the parts of the mine we worked were old and decrepit, already decaying into obsolescence.

He transferred with me to graveyard shift. Graveyard on old seven-fifty, with its quarter sized crew, one shift boss for the whole mine, and a set of

125

unwritten rules that applied only to graveyard. It suited me fine. I liked being the only crew on the level, and only seeing the boss occasionally. I didn't mind having my days turned inside out. At least I didn't have to alternate shifts. Just steady graveyard, going down with the sun and coming back up to see it break over the black rocks of Crean Hill.

He hated it right from the start, but he didn't have enough seniority to bid off, so he was stuck on the motor crew with me, pulling air chutes in the far end of seven-fifty. Oh, I tried to jolly him out of it, but he was scared. He wouldn't admit it but I could see it all right. See, the damn mine was supposed to be haunted. Old Tom they called the ghost. Guys were always telling Old Tom stories. The ghost was only on the upper levels, supposedly. I don't know if any of the stories were true. I did see something once I thought was maybe gas, but it went against the ventilation. Anyway, I shouldn't have told him, because then he was really scared.

It got so it was hard to get him out of the lunch room. He'd lie there on one of the long benches lining the sides of the little screened drift that was the lunch room and he wouldn't get up. It was okay to sleep a bit on graveyard. "Don't let me catch you sleeping," was how the shift boss put it, so he never came down till an hour after lunch. If we had a surprise inspection he would phone us on the old crank phone. "We have visitors." That's all, that was enough.

My partner insisted on pushing the lax rules. He claimed he couldn't sleep at home, not in the daylight, not with the baby awake, and his young wife walking around the house. I'd tell him he couldn't lie there with his head on his lunchpail all shift — we were bound to get caught.

We did get caught, lots of times. The big ventilation doors down by the station would bang, and I'd have to rush him up and into his belt and helmet, but by that time it was too late; the steel fire door would open and there would be Old Snider the shifter, madder than hell. It wasn't my fault, but the old fart always seemed to save his yelling specially for me. Hell, I couldn't carry him.

Look, I guess I believed that the place was haunted. So what! By most of the stories Old Tom was benevolent, or neutral at least. The way I saw it, why would the shade of some long dead miner want to harm me? But I could never get my partner to see it that way. "What did it look like again?" He'd look around, shining his light at the BC timbers as if a ghost might be lurking behind any of them.

I was getting sick of it. "Gas, I told you. It looked like a blue-green ball of gas. Probably was gas."

"But it came down the drift against the ventilation. Didn't you say it went up the manway to the old workings?"

It had, but so what? Ventilation was supposed to go that way. He couldn't be shook loose from it. "But you said it came down the main drift."

"Well, yes." I was trying to get a big stubborn piece of muck into the car. It was stuck on the lip of the chute and I was prying at it with a scaling bar. "But maybe the vent doors were open. Look, take that muck bar and pry this mother over."

He did (he was strong as an ox). The chunk crashed into the steel car below, and he waved his gloved hand at me as if making a big point about my own story. "Yah, but if the doors were open, how'd it go up the manway?"

"Next car!" I said. "How in the hell am I supposed to know?"

I don't know how many times he questioned me about it; the damn ghost was becoming almost his single object of conversation. I'd see him on deck sitting on his upended lunch pail talking to some old timer who was feeding him an Old Tom story that the snuff-chewing old cretin was probably making up on the spot.

He wasn't stupid, and until that time I didn't think he was gullible, but he sure turned out to be. He'd sit in that green painted lunchroom, lean his elbows on his knees and tell me the latest ghost story, with his eyes shining back the reflections of the two light bulbs that the company deemed enough to light our little grotto. "It's all B.S.!" I'd tell him.

He'd get up and pace up and down in those big clumsy miner's boots. "What about the time you saw it?"

Well what about it? I'd see him talking to some clown on deck, and I'd see him gesture toward me and make floating ghost motions with his hands. I knew that he was getting to be a big joke, and dragging me along with him. And why the hell the shift boss or one of the foremen didn't do something about it, is beyond me. Nobody did anything. They just let him go down every night on graveyard to a haunted drift in a slimy cold mine, with a childhood friend who was too callous to help him until it was too late.

It is dark in a mine. You who have never worked

underground know dark only as a rumour. You have never sat on a gangway with the arched black rock above you and turned off your light. A miner learns to look with his whole head. A miner's lamp is his best friend, and when you turn it off, the terrible darkness eats right into you, and the old mine talks to you, and who knows, maybe Old Tom whispers in the back of your brain.

I got him to try it once. God knows what good I thought it would do. I'll bet he didn't have his lamp off for thirty seconds. "You do this for fun?" he whispered.

"Did you hear it?" I don't know why I asked that.

"Hear what?" His voice quivered.

I just smiled, as if I'd heard something unearthly, unmentionable, and not just the unbearable sound of millions of tons of fractured rock settling on top of us.

"What did you hear?" There was a tinge of panic in his voice and I realized I'd gone too far.

I laughed as if it was all a joke, which I guess it was. "Nothing, just the mine talking to us."

It got so that he wanted to blow shifts all the time. I didn't care; I'd stay out with him. It wasn't much fun down there anyway, not with him looking around all the time as if Old Tom was going to reach out through solid rock and drag him down. I'd argue with him. I was single, he was not. He had responsibilities. But no, one shift a week or so we'd be driving into work and he'd say, "Let's stop for a beer." It was never "a" beer. A beer meant that we had two or three. If we said we'd have a "couple," well then my friend, we were not going in to work, because a couple was too much for concentration but not enough to go home until we had a "few." A few made it hard to walk.

Well, we were sitting in the Waters Hotel at one of those little round tables, pouring back the draft with some of the boys from day shift. It was fine for them. They would just be hung over in the morning. We would be short a day's pay, and maybe get another "step" on the way to unemployment. Our cross-shift, George, turned to me, belched, and said "I tried it too."

"Tried what?"

He nodded knowingly. "Listening."

I looked at my partner. "Have you been blabbering all over about that?"

George shook his head. "No, I tried it years before you guys tried it."

My partner leaned over the table. "What did you hear?"

His buddy Roofer scoffed, but George looked glum. "I never did it again, not on the upper levels."

Well you know, it got worse underground with him after that. He blew so many shifts that he had to quit before they fired him. I felt bad about it, of course. He hung around for a few months, and I guess things weren't going too good at home. I did what I could to help, but he was hitting the bottle pretty hard, and finally he just went away. Like I said, I don't know where he went. I haven't heard from him since.

It makes it tricky. See, I moved in with his old lady. She needed somebody, and I always liked her lots. I don't mind the kid. He's as gullible as his old man so he's easy to control. I would marry her, if we could contact him, or if we knew he was dead. I think he's dead. I'll tell you why.

A few months ago, I got to thinking of him and I

turned my light off. His voice was as clear as if he were sitting beside me on the gangway, his voice tinged with panic like it was toward the end—"What did you hear?"

Well I heard him, that's for sure, and I'll tell you one thing. I don't listen like that anymore, not on seven-fifty, not ever.

The Axe

It was a goofy dream, he realized. He knew it was a dream, it felt dreamlike right from the start, cartooney even. The characters in the dream were generic, not anyone that he knew, but familiar, like actors that he had seen on television, or maybe people his mind had generated to be in this fantasy.

They seemed to be shooting a film about something or other, some rare animal perhaps, as the dream was centred in the bush and it involved much walking around little blue lakes or hunting in the deep green spruce. He had argued in the dream, as he would have in reality, that the thick climax forest was not a good spot for moose. He complained but it did no use, as he seemed to be hunting moose here, for some show.

That was it! He was working for some television hunting show. Great job! He must have smiled in reality, sleeping in his bed, because he smiled so hard in the dream that his face ached.

In the dream he shot a moose, a strange caricature of a moose, with pink bubble gum protrusions on its antlers. He stood and looked in amazement at the strange animal.

"Aren't you going to put it out of its misery?" said the female director.

He looked down at the freaky animal; it was lying on its pinkish side with its undersized legs waving uselessly against the duff. Consciousness had already faded from the eyes. "There's no point." He reached for his knife anyway, expecting it to be there in its proper place — after all this was a hunting dream. There was a knife, but it wasn't his; it was dull and useless. The skin of the cartoon moose's neck was unnaturally tough; though he sawed away, feeling foolish, the point wouldn't even penetrate.

"Here." The director held out one of those little Estwing axes. "Use this!"

The camera was rolling, the toy moose was dead, but he hefted the little axe with its steel handle, the sheath was already off, and the padded plastic grip was warm in his hand — there was no doubt that this would do the trick. It seemed expected — maybe an ad? He swung it easily, and it bit cleanly into the neck of the moose.

Fade to consciousness.

That morning, after he had eaten breakfast and checked the cows, he was cleaning up in the workshop and he came upon the little Estwing axe that his wife or kids had got him a few Christmases before. It was a pretty little thing. "A blazing axe," his buddy had called it, "too light for any real work."

He had carried it behind the seat of the farm truck for a while, and had used it once or twice to clear a shooting lane when hunting, but otherwise it just sort of became an addition to the junk behind the seat. At some time or other he had lost the scabbard, and so had stopped carrying it; eventually it had found its way in to the workbench.

He felt the still razor sharp edge, grinned, rolled up his sleeve and shaved a swath of hair off his forearm. "Oh yah, you'd do all right!"

The dream sort of rode on him the next three or four days; it had been a strange and silly dream, not the type of dream he was likely to have at all, and sure enough because it stuck with him he had another version. This time it was a cattle beast, one of his, something was wrong with it, he would have to shoot it, only when he went to get the gun he passed through the workshop, the axe was sitting where he had seen it on the workbench, his guns were locked up, his ammunition was locked up, and he wasn't sure where any clips were, but there was the axe, the animal was in pain and this was a dream, so he went out with the axe. The blow was just above the eyes where a diagonal X would have been formed between the eyes and horns (if the dream angus had had horns—but like a real angus she did not). The axe bit deep into the cow's brain, death was immediate with just a stiffening of legs and a trembling of muscles; the pain was gone.

He stood over his dead cow in the dream and looked in amazement at the axe in his hand. "Wow," he said, "no wonder people used to use these for weapons!"

That got him to thinking on suggestion, and such, and wondering why he dreamed of the axe in the first place, and every time he walked into the workshop he would look at the silvery little axe leaning up against the cupboards on top of the bench. He would have put it back in the truck if he hadn't lost the sheath.

"Damn!" he said. "If I had some leather, I'd make a new one." He hadn't liked the one that came with the axe anyway; it was too flimsy if you actually carried the axe on your belt, and it should have attached lower so the handle of the axe wouldn't hang down quite so low.

He carried the axe into the house and lay it down on stiff paper on the kitchen table, then traced a scabbard around the head, with belt loops running beneath. In the morning he would find a scrap of leather—maybe an old boot—and make a scabbard.

He was in a long dark hallway, nervous, something seemed to be following him; he rounded a climbing corner and came into an underground parking lot, empty, only dim echoing spaces and standing pillars, far walls dim in the distance. Behind him came a shuffling, to the left a faint scrape of sound; he advanced into the centre of the building, something behind him moved. This was a dream, a nightmare! He was having a nightmare, but his heart was pounding like a kid's. What was it he was supposed to do to gain control of a scary dream? "Oh yah!" he said softly, his voice straining against the darkness of the cavernous garage, "look at your hands."

Something sort of man-shaped sloped toward him out of the misty darkness, moaning and gibbering; another was crowding into vision to his left.

"Look at your hands!" he said into the monster's

face, then tore his eyes away from it and looked
down—there were his hands and in them was the
Estwing axe. "Ha ha ha ha ha!" he giggled in the thing's
face before driving the axe blade into its head, clean to
the handle. It slumped at his feet; the other thing
turned and ran. "Come back and play, " he hollered
after it; "I'll show you my axe."

"To hell with this!" he said in the morning. "I don't
need a letter straight from God. I'm taking you with
me." He picked up the little axe, and carried it out to
the truck, intending to wrap it in an old coat that was
behind the seat, but the coat was missing, used for
some other chore no doubt, so he shoved the sharp
head in the wrist part of a dirty leather glove. "There,
that will keep you and me both safe for now, until I
build you a sheath."
    He never quite got that done over the next couple
of days, but he didn't dream of the axe any more either,
as if having it ride behind him on his round of chores
was what it wanted all the time. He never used it of
course, and he would have made the sheath
eventually—he did cut out his pattern and find a good
old work boot that he had kept around for that
purpose—but before he could find his leather awl he
rolled his truck on the corner that swung around the
lake just before his other place. Though not wearing
his seatbelt he would have been alright—the truck
skidded on the snowy road, and he almost caught it
turning into the skid, but the rear bumper ploughed
though the snowbank, caught on a guard rail, and
rolled the half ton over and over down the gravel. He'd
lived through worse accidents and he was pretty

sure—the sky was going over and over, and he was getting bounced around in slow motion—he was alright in this one. It was only at the last moment that he saw the unsheathed axe in front of his face.

Gardenia's Garden

Over near the edge of the bluff is an old house, apple trees in the front where you drive up. A rotten looking old step threatens to buckle under your unexpected weight, but the screen door opens into a vestibule larder and from there into the clanking kitchen.

Gardenia's there, but if you stand out on the back step she'll never hear you, unless you bellow like a maniac—you got to walk in that porch and knock on the kitchen screen door. Take your boots off; you are about to get invited in. I can't imagine who Gardenia wouldn't invite in, certainly nobody that's ever come to her door yet.

It's okay, just walk up the steps, don't you worry about the social conventions, Gardenia's gonna like you just fine, there is no reason she wouldn't, she likes everyone. Nobody will think anything of it, she's always got visitors, often someone down on their luck—knock on the door.

Here's what I want you to do: look right in my eyes,

and get up and walk with me, it's just a little way, right on the edge of this bluff. You've seen it from the highway — an old barn and outbuildings and this little white house right on the edge of the bluff. It's right down the road.

Of course, if you're going to stay you'll have to work in Gardenia's garden; I can think of worse jobs — the sun shining down and the view going on over little farms and spruce bush and hardwood ridges running along the sides. Where have you got to go that's better than that?

You must be empty; Gardenia will fill you up, on roast goose and wild rice, on moose steaks and mashed potatoes, honeyed carrots. She'll feed you other ways too; you need some time with Gardenia.

You tell Gardenia I sent you, if it makes you feel any better about it; she'll ask you if I did anyway. I never could get one over on her. She won't care if you're in trouble, you won't be no trouble there, and no one can find you.

Don't you worry about after either, she'll fix you up, and when she's done, and next winter's wood is in the shed, and a pig, a buck and a beef are hanging in the smoker or pickling in the basement, you'll be fine. Gardenia will set you up with something to do.

Religion? I guess it's sort of religious all right, but not like you think — she won't preach at you or anything. She sings some, real pretty, but it's not really religious, not in the way, say, church or the Jehovah's Witnesses are, or anything. If it's a religion it doesn't need no book or teaching; it just is.

Don't worry about stuff any more, you got to get past doing that, none of that matters, it's all moved on. I know that the car looks all wrecked and still, but it's moving on, and you're going down that apple-lined drive to Gardenia's garden.

It'll be nice. Knock on the door. Tell her I sent you.

Note on the Author

Charlie Smith was born in Blind River, Ontario in 1948. His mother Iona Hamilton of Spanish, Ontario wrote poetry, as did her father Charlie Hamilton, also of Spanish. Charlie's father, Charles T. Smith was from Illinois, and Charlie was "shook round this continent / Like a pebble in a can," attending public school in Silver Water, Ont., Rockford, Ill., Elizabeth Bay, Ont., Grand Detour, Ill., Spanish, Ont., Grand Detour, Ill. (again), and Evansville, Ont. He went to High School in Orangeville, Ont., and Gore Bay, Ont., where he graduated with his grade 12 diploma. He married his wife Rhonda Lane just out of high school, and spent 10 years in the INCO mines in Sudbury. He and Rhonda then bought their home — christened Earthfast — on the Birch Lake Road, northeast of Massey, Ont., where Charlie fulfilled his dream of being "A father, a farmer, a good rifle shot." They have three children, Rebecca, Chuck, and Brandon, and three grandchildren, Maeve, Angus and Nora Elizabeth.

Tag Alder Tales follows Charlie's two successful YSPress collections of poetry: *The Beast that God has Kissed: Songs from the Birch Lake Road,* and *Through Three Long Miles of Night: More Songs from the Birch Lake Road.* The gift for narrative so evident in those poems manifests itself richly in this first collection of stories.